SEX IN MEDICINE

"The secret side of Health Care"

OBSERVATIONS OF A DISENCHANTED, DISGUSTED AND DEMORALISED DOCTOR

Dr.
French

Fifi

DISCLAIMER

The stories written are dramatizations inspired by actual events. Certain scenes, dialogue and characters have been enhanced for dramatic purposes. Some archival material is referred to.

The intention is not to offend or ridicule as the manuscript refers only loosely to living and dead people unless facts are in the public domain. Factual events have often been dramatized for literary purpose. The true and shocking stories are available on the internet.

PROLOGUE

I write this semi-fictional novel as a sequel to my first novel "Murder in Medicine" available from Amazon books on-line or on my webpage https//fififrench.co.uk

THE MAIN CHARACTERS IN 'MURDER IN MEDICINE' ARE

Fifi French- doctor of medicine

Yvan Cohen –her life partner

Maria- his house keeper

Renee- a bridge player and good friend

BBO -In the time of Corona virus the bridge players use an online facility for playing bridge . The App is Bridge base on line –BBO. Before that bridge players frequented bridge clubs to play games

Background to Murder in Medicine

Fifi gave up practising medicine to write her book -Murder in Medicine documenting the wrongs that she saw in her years in Health care. Yvan helped her with the book. This won him a place in her heart. He is an older man with a left sided paralysis which developed while playing bridge. Despite the stroke, Fifi finds him enormously attractive and fun to be with.

Doctors in Fifi's opinion range from good to mediocre to bad. Fifi did partake in some of the sexual frivolities mentioned.   Her activities were harmless, driven by burgeoning hormones in a young pretty woman with naturally good breasts and legs.

Fifi saw and heard lots of sexual gossip and encountered some events herself. Basic details of what happened to patients and staff are correct. The rest is fictionalised and did not happen. Internet reference allows the reader to be shocked by the truth of some events and what actually happened

DEDICATION

THIS BOOK IS DEDICATED TO ALL THE SEX MAD DOCTORS AND HEALTH CARE STAFF I HAVE MET THROUGH MY LIFE. THERE HAVE BEEN MANY

MY ADVICE TO THEM IS – MEN -KEEP IT IN YOUR PANTS AND SEEK COUNSELLING

-LADIES –JUST DON'T DO IT.

IF THIS BOOK TEACHES YOU ANYTHING YOU DIDN'T KNOW. PLEASE DON'T ACT ON IT. YOU WILL GET INTO TROUBLE AND MAY GO TO JAIL. SOMEONE CAN HELP YOU

Perversion is a type of human behaviour that deviates from that which is understood to be orthodox or normal. Although the term **perversion** can refer to a variety of forms of deviation, it is most often used to describe sexual behaviours that are considered particularly abnormal, repulsive or obsessive.

The underlying cause of male acts of perversion has always been explained as the need for control and mastery in order to compensate for deep-seated feelings of sexual insecurity, which in turn are caused by arrested psychosexual development.

You can be perverted, but if it stays in your head, it can't be considered **wrong**. It might cause you pain if you feel like you have an ugly secret or believe no one will ever love the real you. Whatever you feel, there are people out there who understand you because they feel the same things.

Always seek help. Do not seek to foster, enhance or act on your perversion. Try and understand it and control it.

CONTENTS

1   THE FEMALE PREDATOR

"I lied. I don't need Viagra"

"So I noticed."

Fi was lying across Yvan, all parts of her female anatomy in direct contact with him. Her neck curled into his chest, head buried in his open necked shirt luxuriating in the silk cravat he wore and his masculine smell. Yvan's paralysed left arm lying comfortably across her upper body felt the curves of her back, elbow conscious of her buttock into which it pressed. Fi, not erotically driven, noted the hardness pressing into her thighs. Yvan does not mention it.

"I am glad you will not permit me to have sex with you. Perhaps when you are a Babushka"

"No never" Fifi sang out the line from the Texas lightning song. "Not till we get married"

"Are all you Asian female doctors the same?"

"Do you mean Asian by genealogy or by cultural upbringing?"

"Why? Is there a difference in behaviour? You are all repressed."

"Not so; I can tell you this amazing story of a Canadian Asian female doctor Theepa Sundaralingam and what she did. Her name sounds culturally like an Asian Tamil. She looks Asian Tamil but the one video clip I saw of her shows her speaking with a non-Asian accent. Third generation Canadian I guess. She too,like all the doctors I read about was insane; sexually forward.”

Fi could feel Yvan’s tumescence decrease as he concentrated on what she was saying.

“I read it in the Toronto press. I’ll show you her picture. So pretty, 37 years old; talented; a consultant oncologist. I think I know what happened with her and the patient whose name isn’t mentioned in the newspaper article.”

Yvan gently moved Fi off him. ”I am practically drowned by your body. I’d rather be on top of you though, or inside you.”

“I call her Thioteepa. It’s a hominim. Thiotepa is a cancer drug and her name Theepa, very similar to that cancer drug name and she chooses cancer as her speciality. Theepa‘s behaviour is madness personified. Imagine yourself as the patient. Let’s call him Vittorio”

Yvan lay back, eyes closed, listening

“Vittorio is lying there in his hospital bed on the oncology ward. He has been admitted urgently for a diagnosis of testicular cancer. He is anxious. He sees this vision of loveliness walking towards him. It is Thioteepa.”

“Hi Vittorio; I’m Dr Sundaralingam. Forget that name call me Theepa”

She gives him the standard doctor chit chat. Takes the story of how he noticed this lump and what his symptoms are. She forms a bond with him. Who wouldn’t? He is young and handsome; lean with dark curly hair and slightly tanned skin. He oozes masculinity.

He is worried about having a cancer. She reassures him. She is nice to him gently touching his arm as she talks.

He takes more notice of this dusky skinned Asian beauty than of what she is saying. He notes her short skirt and open white blouse showing a hint of cleavage below the diamante necklace. He relaxes.

Thioteepa thinks 'Gorgeous guy.'

"Can you take your pants off and show me the lump? I have to examine you now."

Vittorio looks embarrassed but this is a doctor not a young woman who has managed to charm him. It is absurd but he is getting involved emotionally. He looks at her uncertainly but admiringly as he takes off his corduroy trousers and his boxer shorts temporarily forgetting the death threat of cancer.

"Lie down again for the examination."

She crosses to the sink and washes her hands in warm water. She warms them so they don't feel cold on his skin. He notes her pert buttock accentuated by the high heels as she moves. You could almost see the cleft through the thin skirt. He thinks 'Do doctors wear thongs to work?'

She comes back and touches him moving her warm hands slowly over the testicle and lump.

He grows big. Thioteepa thinks; 'Ohh; large and beautiful to look at.' She is not embarrassed. She concentrates on it rather than the lump. Accidentally or deliberately she touches it. It grows larger. She spends about 20 minutes examining the area.

He doesn't say anything about his erection. He is proud of it. A sign of his virility in the face of a possible emasculation by treatment. Castration was suggested to him as part of the cancer treatment discussed with him by his referring doctor. He is a young man and a beautiful woman is softly pressing the rugosa of his scrotum while examining him. She takes longer than she should; enjoying the look and feel of playing with his genitals and using it as an excuse to be close to the engorgement. He finally presses on the top of his erection while she continues her examination. He is trying to prevent himself ejaculating.

The footsteps of the nurse are heard coming towards the room. Thioteepa says, smiling at Vittorio her hand passing over the erection and his hand "You can get dressed now. I'll refer you for removal of the lump and a whole body CT and see you afterwards for treatment and follow up."

He hides his tumescence under the bed covers as the nurse enters, flattening it hard with his hand.

"I will give you my personal attention Vittorio so don't worry. Let me know whatever happens to you. Text me whenever you come to hospital for treatment. Here is my mobile phone number. After she leaves he thinks of Theepa and strokes himself gently then faster till release.

Yvan, putting his hands in his trousers to adjust himself said

"Ohhh. Did that really happen?"

"Of course not; I have no idea. Nothing like that was in the Toronto press report. They didn't even give his name. All they said was that she formed a relationship with him and on one occasion she texted him asking him whether he had ever been to a cheese and porn party"

"OMG. You doctors have a good life."

"I have never been to a cheese and porn party Yvan; neither have I been invited to any. Maybe they only happen in Canada?"

"Was she a sexy lady. What else did she do?"

"She was sex mad and frustrated Yvan. Good doctors don't do that kind of thing with attractive patients. I didn't. "

"What else happened?"

"She obviously liked to live dangerously. When Vittorio comes into hospital for a blood transfusion.,," Yvan interrupts her hastily

"No, no describe it like a story. It's more exciting." Yvan was sensuously wallowing in the moment. Fi could see he was aroused. "What do men do with boners? I've wanted to ask you for ages."

"They usually massage it. In case they are missing something" Fi said good humouredly noticing what Yvan was doing and saying

"I do know that Fi but I'm holding out till you are my wife."

"I'll tell you the story instead. You carry on with the good exercise for your paralysed arm. I presume your maid has gone to bed?"

"She doesn't provide that type of service Fi, although I must admit I've never asked her" Yvan laughed. "I don't really like her flat as a pancake features. She looks like a Babushka. She's gone home." He pulls Fi closer to him. "Put your leg over me Feef." Fi obliges, covering his thighs with her right leg. She continues her story. She closes her eyes imagining the scene in Toronto and recounting it.

Thioteepa finishes her clinic quickly. She washes herself and drowns her armpits in "Poison" from Ralph Lauren. A few drops go into her underwear.

Her relationship with Vittorio has progressed to flirting and texting with sexual innuendo. She is excited by the intimacy

Vittorio is sitting on the day-ward having a blood transfusion. His cancer chemotherapy treatments are progressing well. He is waiting eagerly for Thioteepa

Theepa knows Vittorio is coming to hospital that day because she has received a text message from him. She dresses especially sexily knowing he will notice. Today she has fish net stockings under her short skirt. Her doctor's jacket covers a see-through blouse. She has calf length ankle boots.

Arriving on the day-ward she chats to the nurses at the nursing station, not going to Vittorio's bedside straight away. He is watching her as he sits in the low armchair beside his bed. His left arm has the drip-tubing with blood dripping slowly. His right arm is free.

Theepa approaches, smiling her devastating smile. She pulls the curtains round the bed to give them privacy. She sits on the edge of the bed. She notices him looking at her legs and starts chatting to him. She opens her legs slightly while chatting. He looks from his position in the armchair up her spread thighs and notices her black lace underwear and the swells of her thighs plump and luscious above the stocking tops.

"Are you wearing a thong?" he whispers

"Feel for yourself" she whispers back

She takes his right hand and places it on her thigh. She moves forward on the bed so his fingers can get under the edge and probe deeper. She stands up so he can achieve full entry. She doesn't flinch as he uses three fingers. Her breath is coming in soft gasps as he is doing this. She tries not to moan. She leans forward and holds him through his track suit bottom stroking his visible hardness. He brings his other hand up to her blouse through which he can clearly see her arousal. He squeezes the protruding points

They hear footsteps outside. "Be careful of the cannula into which the blood is going Vittorio. The nurses won't want to reposition it" she says moving away quickly.

She pulls back the bed curtains and goes to talk to the nurse outside acting very professionally and normally. He is left with his erection and the smell of her on the fingers of his right hand.

Yvan moaned "Wasn't she afraid of being caught?"

"They didn't discuss that aspect in the newspaper report. All they said was that the contact occurred."

Yvan laughed. "The heady excitement of dangerous, illicit sex."

Fi put her hand into Yvan's lap covering his hand"Yes dangerously so but it heightens the excitement. You and I, here, kinda boring with no one else around. If your maid was here we would have the potential fear of discovery."

"How did all this come to light with Theepa? They seem to have hidden it well"

"Thiotepa progresses on to having a stolen sexual relationship with Vittorio. Visiting his home for sex and still continuing to manage his medical case. This was the wrong doing Yvan. If she had wanted to have a relationship she should have transferred his care to someone else."

"Can you do that?"

"Doctors are human and some can fall in love with their patients. In these cases you should step out of the professional role, discuss what has happened with your superiors and stop looking after the patient. Not do both. It gives the patient a supposed fairer deal without the emotionalism clouding judgement on clinical decisions that are made"

"What happened to her? Did she follow that protocol?"

"No. She continued the relationship and his clinical care until she fell in love with someone else. She then tried to terminate her relationship with Vittorio. He as a jilted lover reported her to the authorities. Strangely they made Thiotepa pay compensation not only to Vittorio but to her professional body"

"She doesn't sound like a sexual predator?"

"No just stupid, lustful and frustrated. When did you pounce on anyone at the bridge club?"

"Never. Just hid my urges till you came along." Yvan moved away from Fi and stood up. "I'm tired of sitting in the couch but I don't want to tear myself away from the touch and feel of you. Let's go to bed and you can complete what you started Fi. Sleep beside me tonight."

"Ok but only to read out what happened to Thiotepa and the story that was in the press. No hanky panky."

"Aaah what a hard bargain you drive" They walked upstairs to the third floor of the house. Yvan took his time negotiating the stairs. Fi was washed undressed to her bra and panties and tucked under the burgundy silk covers when he finally arrived.

 "Here's the story in 'The Canadian press'" she said. Yvan had finished his nightly ablutions. He got into bed smelling of toothpaste and soap. His pyjamas were silk burgundy. He took his black rimmed glasses off and placed them on the mahogany bed table. Fi read the Google article out to him

Toronto doctor Theepa Sundaralingam sent flirty texts to a patient newly diagnosed with cancer in January 2015, according to an uncontested statement of facts. The affair began with flirtatious texts.

"Have u ever been to a porn and cheese party?" Sundaralingam wrote in one of the texts to the patient on March 3, 2015. "Oh wait, I don't think that's a normal activity — my bad."

Those texts escalated to sex and masturbation in the hospital where he was receiving treatment for cancer, including one night where she slept in the patient's bed.

Yvan moaned.

"Describe it as a story Fi. She certainly is a thrill seeker. How does she get past the nurses?"

"I have no idea. I'll try and imagine how. Maybe Canadian wards are different to British? Cuddle up to me. I'm cold. My feet are freezing"

The night nurses have taken over from the day staff and the last observations have been done on Vittorio for that day. As an experienced hospitalised patient, he knows he will not be disturbed after that.

Thiotepa as a consultant knows that although it is not her night on-call the nurses will not be surprised if she arrives late to talk about her patients. The nurses won't challenge her.

 She arrives on the ward, talks to them says goodnight to the nurses half hour later and as she leaves the ward appears to change her mind going to an open bay where another oncology patient is. She chats to that patient and then pretends to leave the ward but doubles back and slips into Vittorio's room.

Vittorio has showered. He is lying in bed naked except for his underpants.

Thiotepa says nothing. She approaches the bed in silence and very slowly starts undressing. She knows how to do it. The white doctor's jacket comes off first. Her stethoscope is in its pocket. She places it noiselessly on the chair by his bed. As she unfastens the buttons on her blouse he can see the raised dark points of arousal. She takes her blouse off. Her lacy leopard skin diaphanous bra is removed. She leans over him angling her left breast towards his mouth. He sucks and moves to the other in quick succession.

She moves back moaning softly unzips her skirt pulls back the bedclothes and scantily clad as she has nothing but her matching thong , sits astride him moving his Y fronts down. With both pieces of underwear still partly in place she rides him. She dominates him till he finishes and then says

"I should go now"

"Did you come?" he asks

She smiles shaking her head "Just a small one"

"Sit astride my face" he says. She moves up to his face. Soft slurping sounds drown out her rapid breathing. She finishes herself on his tongue within seconds. By this time he is ready again. He entraps both her hands above her head and gets on top of her. He keeps his lips over her mouth all the time to prevent her from moaning. He comes again, hips banging into her.

"So nice to have sex without a condom" she says

Vittorio laughs "One of the advantages of having both your rugby balls removed."

"Can you get erections after your testes are removed?" Yvan questioned

"Yes but you can never have children. The rest of the system works normally."

Vittorio and Thiotepa fall asleep in each other's arms for a short while

It's the early hours of the morning. Light has not yet peeped through the chinks of the hospital curtain. Vittorio awakes and enters her once more from behind fast and forcefully. He has exhausted her. "I must leave she says before we get caught"

She gets up and walks to the bathroom door. "Make sure you strip your bed and leave the sheets on the floor for them to make your bed today. Otherwise you will be found out." He opens the hospital bedroom door slightly and peers round it. Theepa with her shoes in hand, in her bare feet follows behind him. He looks out and sees that the coast is clear. He signals her while keeping a look out and she slips off the ward.

Throughout the story Fi could hear Yvan's hand, busy rhythmically moving under the bed covers.

She smiles at him mischievously and says "Should I ask you Vittorio's question to Thiotepa?" Yvan doesn't answer. His movements are getting faster and then he groans and grunts in release.

The next morning at breakfast Fi read out the rest of the newspaper article to him

Theepa asked the patient to alter hospital documents to hide the affair, the statement of facts said.

"Almost instantly after diagnosing Patient A with a life-altering diagnosis, Dr. Sundaralingam began to breach well established boundaries between physicians and patients,"

"This was all with the knowledge that what she was doing was wrong. The evidence makes clear that she asked Patient A to falsify hospital documents in order to conceal her abuse. Only revocation can maintain confidence in the medical profession's ability to regulate itself."

Theepa would often stay with the patient for hours while he was at the hospital for chemotherapy. She performed blood transfusions on him and the pair also touched each other sexually, the statement of facts said. In one visit after she examined the patient she asked the patient to examine her. He complied.

"Oh lord, its breakfast and it is sex. The maid will arrive soon and you are making me desirous again Fi; adults playing doctor. I thought that was only a game children indulged in"

"Do you like fantasy role playing Yvan? We can play doctor-nurse if you do."

Yvan shakes his head in dissent. "No fantasy for me. Just a wife to have sex with."

"You are permitted to return upstairs for fear of Maria's discovery Yvan, but the sex side of Theepa is nearly over. Now it gets to how she got into this terrible trouble."

Yvan concentrates on his cereal trying to keep his thoughts off sexy doctors. His useful hand is on the table grabbing his cereal bowl.

Vittorio and Thioteepa had sex in the hospital on two occasions and also engaged in sexual activities when she visited him at his family home for treatment.

In September 2016, seven months after the affair started, she has sex with Vittorio at the patient's home, then tells him she is in love with a colleague. Their sexual relationship ended. By November 2016 she refused to see him.

The development was "devastating" he wrote in a victim impact statement.

"Dr. Sundaralingam was the person who both managed my health and provided me with emotional support during cancer treatment," he wrote. "She was the same person who abandoned me at my most vulnerable point. I was physically emaciated and emotionally exposed and the loss of a critical relationship defeated me."

Fi looked angry. "What a bitch she is. He is losing weight. Losing his attractiveness as extremely thin people often do, and she turns her affection to someone else more attractive and exciting."

"I know what you mean Fi, like those awful pictures of a thin Celine Dion in the news?"

"Yes exactly like that. Many people thought Celine looked so ugly and emaciated with her weight loss but Vittorio is suffering cancer weight loss poor fellow. Not a lot he can do about it. He loses his attractiveness and she goes on to greener pastures. Emotionally ruthless women like her should never be allowed to work again."

The patient said he didn't understand the ramifications of the relationship with his doctor, nor did he understand his vulnerability.

"There was an imbalance of power in the relationship because of my dependence on her for both medical care and emotional and sexual intimacy," he wrote. The patient also said he has seen a psychologist for treatment.

Sundaralingam was ordered to pay $16,000 towards the patient's therapy and $6,000 in costs to the college.

Yvan said "They didn't stop her from continuing to practice?" Fi shook her head. "And her payment costs would have been met by her defence organisation so she suffered nothing. Just loss of face from her elders and perhaps gained kudos with her peers for her sexual high jinks.

 Laughing Yvan said "Which hospital did you say she was working at? Maybe she'll like to have sex with a guy who has had a stroke? I'll give permission so long as she wears her doctor's jacket throughout."

" That is far to travel for a pronging Yvan; to Ontario. Although that gay television presenter, what was his name? Gary something or other did say that gay guys would travel long distances for sex."

"Mmm I've heard that too"

"I however think her perk was because she could live dangerously. My second child was conceived from antics in a car on Fleet Street. That's the maximum danger I ever achieved.

2. **THE FLASHER**

Yvan was walking back from the toilet when Fi noticed that his trouser zip was undone. She laughingly said "Put it away Yvan. The other female bridge players at the club tonight will want some of it"

He looked down, saw what she was referring to and said "Tis only for you dear heart but I'm glad you pointed it out. I wouldn't want to be accused of flashing even though I am proud of its size and length."

"Those come in all shapes and sizes and some people are unfortunately born with two appendages."

"Yes.I know. Steve sent round an almost pornographic video with a guy using both. He sent it on Whatsapp. I blocked him after that"

"The medical term is diphallia- two appendages. I did the same thing; blocked Steve from Facebook as well. He is sick. He thought it was an advantage having two, one for each orifice. I told him being born with a deformity like Marilyn Monroe's six toes is not an advantage in life. Obsessed with a...holes because he is one."

"He probably could be a flasher."

"No too disgusting. The only flasher doctor I knew was terribly sweet, played cello in an orchestra in the North of England and no one would have believed it of him. He was caught, arrested and charged and never went back to medicine. He is dead now aged 80. I would have looked at it for him anytime. He only needed to ask. He never flashed at work. Just on the alleyways of North England"

Renee had walked into the bar at the bridge club. Overhearing the conversation she said "I read about a flasher doctor once. He had an Asian name and worked in the North. Was that him?"

 "No the guy I knew was English although I know who you mean."

"These Asian doctors are all the same" Yvan said irritably. "What's up with their sexuality?"

"You are right Yvan most of the sexually inappropriate stories are about ethnically non-Caucasian doctors. I think the false myths of holiness in their religion. It prevents the expression of their sexuality. That is the problem; and their culture. Religion, upbringing and pretend morality mean they can't reveal their desires. They are sexually repressed"

Renee said "I'm happy to give them a free encounter any day. At the moment no one has sex with me. I'm too fat"

"Renee; too much information. Which flashing doctor did Renee mean Fi?"

"Dr Mohammad Ihsan. He was suspended from working after he offered to have sex with one patient on his surgery desk. At the time he claimed he was 'sorry' for his actions and enlisted the service of a mentor so he could express his 'regret and awareness' at his behaviour."

"So he wasn't a flasher? Just a sex crazed doctor?"

"Hang on I'll get to that bit. Note his name. The guy is a Muslim and he is married."

Ihsan, from Huddersfield, was then reported to police over claims he made sexual advances to his housekeeper and exposed himself to her.

No criminal action was taken but his case went before the General Medical Council (GMC) and Ihsan was found guilty of sexually motivated misconduct and taken off from the medical register.

"Stupid to lose your job for sex."

"I'll tell you about Jonathon Fielden and other sex crazed doctors who lose their livelihood for sex Yvan but what I can't believe is the GMC. You've heard my views on how they operate and who they permit to work after a disciplinary hearing. When I tell you what happened with Dr Ihsan's patients you will wonder why he was ever allowed to work after that and offend once more.

"The GMC don't get it right."Yvan said. "I know that from the cases in your book 'Murder in Medicine'"

"Ihsan obviously was a pervert but when you pretend to the GMC to be apologetic they let the doctor continue to work and commit more offences. It's the GMC's formulaic approach to how to deal with issues. That's what makes their decisions, unreal."

A Medical Practitioners Tribunal was told that patients made complaints about Ihsan following consultations in February and July 2016 at the Church View Health Centre in South Kirkby near Wakefield whilst he was working as a locum.

"Ah the dreaded locum doctor strikes again" Yvan said

"Not when I was a locum Yvan. No irregularities as a locum from me. Some locums do and some don't. I cannot remember a single sexual encounter as a locum."

"You are too damned virtuous Fi"

"That's your libido talking Yvan and that's what got Ihsan into trouble"

The first complainant to report Ihsan said he began talking about her sex life when she asked him for antibiotics for a chest infection.

In a statement, she said: 'He started by asking me if I was sexually active or if I had a sex life and I responded by saying no I don't really have a sex life, I am menopausal so don't really feel like it and my husband is fine with that. But he then began to ask me questions about my husband asking how I satisfy him and what would I do if he was feeling sexual.

'Dr Ihsan then asked me how I would pleasure my husband and I responded by saying manually. I felt uncomfortable and I tried to get back on to my symptoms rather than answering his questions.'

The woman said Ihsan became more 'explicit and irrelevant' and asked her about her orgasms. She later reported the matter to the health centre.

The second woman saw the doctor for a review about her contraception and he told her: 'I can tell you are in a good place - you look good.'

In her statement, the second complainant said: 'Dr Ihsan then moved his chair towards to me and said 'I'm horny me'.

I made him repeat what he had said because I thought I was hearing things. He went on to tell me how to really be healthy by having sex, lots. He said I was beautiful and I had soft skin. He then touched my right cheek with his left hand.'

She reminded him he had patients waiting outside, but he replied: "I can lock the door if you want me to". He added: "I can tell you look after yourself by looking at your nails. I want to show you something, I want you to see my balls - I really, really want you to see my balls". He then offered to clear his desk and have sex on it.'

"There is the flasher bit coming out Yvan and as a Muslim why didn't he just have 4 wives? Show it to all of them in sequence? What makes him think he can talk to a patient like that?"

Renee intrigued, questioned "What does the Quran tell you about showing your parts to others who don't want to see them?"

Fi said "Ha ha Renee. I'll ask my Muslim friends. I won't mention the names of all the bridge players who have wanted me to watch them on webcam who weren't Muslim."

Renee looked shocked

"They are from all over the world Renee. I have no idea why they want to show it to other bridge players. One guy sent me a photograph of himself on Messenger. He was naked with the top showing; non erect. The text photo he sent was of someone going down on a woman. I blocked him after that sick shieet.""

"Renee pretend whispered to Fi "Give me all their names later" They both laughed a full minute.

 Ihsan admitted ten charges but denied 21 others. He was found guilty of sexually motivated misconduct towards the second woman but a disciplinary panel found his conduct towards the first complainant was not sexually motivated.

"This is why I think these people on the panel hearings lack judgement because they are not medical. " Renee shot her a knowing look

"If you complain of a chest infection nothing should be discussed about your sex life unless you are talking about a genital infection such as Candida- vaginal thrush"

"He wanted to have some sexual encounter Fi but was that all? Wanting to show his rugby tackle to the second patient?" Yvan's curiosity surfaced

"No. He gets another job and 'bingo' he does it again but not with a patient this time. He thinks it is permissible if it's kept out of the consulting room."

"As a family doctor he kept his job after the first complaint despite making sexual advances towards the patient. That is what the GMC allows. All because he pretends to be apologetic. They leave him in this position of power and he exposes himself to a second woman whilst taking a shower at his apartment.

"What he should have done was get help shouldn't he?"

"True. In April 2017 when Ihsan moved to Kings Lynn, Norfolk to take up a job at Queen Elisabeth Hospital, he exposed himself to the housekeeper whilst she was retrieving cleaning items from her trolley.

The woman claimed he locked the door to the flat then pushed her into a corner before dropping his towel and grabbing her bottom. She said she managed to break free when her mobile phone rang and she unlocked the door before escaping.

Ihsan admitted wearing nothing but a towel in front of the housekeeper but was cleared of making sexual advances towards her.

He denied being a 'serial abuser' and claimed he was a 'good and useful doctor who got on well with patients and colleagues.'

Yvan and Renee, both sucked in their breaths simultaneously. Renee exploded, her breasts heaving as she laughed at what Yvan said "Good at what? Exposing ball bearings?"

Of the incident with the housekeeper Ihsan told the hearing: 'I told her I needed to go out and asked if she would mind if I had a shower... I asked about a shower in part to gauge her reaction.'

"Gauge her reaction to what? His erection? The size, shape, or colour? Maybe he wanted her to feel it and test the meat?" Yvan's nostrils flared disdainfully

 Mirth overtook them all. "Yvan have you ever wanted to show your parts on webcam or real life?" Renee asked

"Let me have a look Yvan. I haven't seen any real ones for a long while." They both started laughing. "Fi I do need the list of all the bridge players who want to show their parts. Say I'll visit in person." Fi, smilingly continued

The tribunal's panel chairman Jane Wheat said: 'The Tribunal had regard to the additional information about Dr Ihsan's previous GMC history, in particular, the previous finding of sexually motivated conduct.

'It concluded that having had two adverse findings of sexually motivated conduct, on two occasions less than a year apart, demonstrated Dr Ihsan's lack of appreciation of sexual boundaries. Erasure from the medical register is the appropriate and proportionate outcome in this case to mark the seriousness"

"Wish he was my doctor" Renee said "I'd swing from the chandeliers with him."

The conversation was interrupted by hysterical fits exploding from both as Yvan said "They would break Renee and you'd fall flat on your face."

"Are the flashers mainly ethnic and young or if they are English like your guy are they old?"

"I don't know about the statistic Yvan but let me think of the names of the flashers that I know of"

 In Oakland a radiologist was charged with exposing himself twice in the parking lot at a popular shopping mall in Rochester Hills.

Abizer Sakarwala a radiologist at Beaumont Royal Oak was accused of exposing himself while in his 2003 Lexus in the parking lot of the Village of Rochester Hills in at least two separate instances one month apart.

"The cretin drives a Lexus and loses his job for exposing? Why doesn't he just employ a prossie and wiggle it around if he can afford an expensive car like that?

Fi's mirth was apparent "He wanted a cheap thrill. There are other sex mad morons around." Reading her mind and knowing another story was going to surface, Yvan gave Fi a quizzical eyebrow,

"Jeffrey Zapora. A surgical resident at Lehigh Valley Health Network was accused of repeatedly exposing himself in Lehigh County. It was reported while I was in America on LehighValleyLive.com. He appeared in court on three counts of indecent exposure -- two at Muhlenberg College and the other at a local Wawa.

"Did he drive a Lexus as well?"

"I wouldn't mind if they were in a Ford fiesta Yvan. I've never seen a flasher. Do flashers want a certain sort of person to look at their boners? Was I not good enough?

"That is such a good question Renee. Must look up the answer or have you just been lucky?"

"Unlucky, you mean, "she retorted. They were both chortling "My expectations have never been met" Renee said. "Have I been in the wrong place at the wrong time?"

Fi looked up 'Victims of flashers on a google search'

Victims of flashers are primarily female, and they don't receive much sympathy. The perceived idea is that when a flasher flashes, the victim can wryly comment that she's seen a bigger one on the end of a cocktail stick, and he'll slink away shamed. Another myth is that flashing is the preserve of sad old men who haven't had their end away for some time and are indulging in some innocent fun.

She looked up at Renee. "You've been in the right place Renee. That's why you've never come across a flasher. Schoolgirls are a common target"

"Why do people worry about flashers Fi?" The intellectual side of Yvan had surfaced.

"If a big man confronts a lone female walking her spaniel through woods, the fear is paralysing. For most women the sight of a penis isn't the problem. The problem is, will he attack her? He has already proved that he is prepared to cross the boundaries of normal conduct."

"Do they become rapists?"

"No. Today's flasher is tomorrow's flasher. These guys find flashing itself rewarding. They have fantasies about what their victim is imagining. They have persuaded themselves that their victim is aroused by the sight of their penis. If they had more direct contact with the victim, they would be swiftly disabused of this belief. That's why they keep their distance."

"What treatment is available. Does treatment work?"

"A more radical - and reportedly very successful - approach has been pioneered by clinical psychiatrists in the United States. A row of female volunteers are lined up in the clinic and the flasher is told to expose himself in front of them. "They all stand there poker-faced and don't respond at all. This is very traumatic for the bloke and he never wants to do it again. It changes the meaning that flashing has for him."

"So it's the response of the victim that makes them continue to flash Renee. Your response would probably put them off"

Renee smiled. "I would pounce Fi. That would put them off for life"

"Tackle the flasher to the ground Renee" Yvan said. "Damage them physically"

"Well Yvan sometimes people are accused falsely and then you will be held up for assault. Dr Adeniran Yesufu was accused of carrying out indecent exposure at Nottingham City Hospital three times in late 2007 and early 2008 in a smoking area but a General Medical Council (GMC) fitness to practise panel decided eyewitness evidence did not prove that it was Dr Yesufu who was responsible. As a number of the sightings had taken place in poor lighting and weather conditions they couldn't be certain.

"Did he or didn't he" Yvan asked.

"I'll leave you to be the judge of that Yvan. Images from the CCTV camera didn't identify it as him"

"I'm here waiting to see it" Renee cried. "Why don't they show it to me? I've never met a flasher; doctor or no doctor. Need to get my schoolgirl outfit out."

Yvan understood what she wasn't saying. He reached over his good right arm and hugged her. "Sorry Renee I'm spoken for. Can't show you mine"

"I commend your professionalism Yvan but one quick peek won't be harmful"

 Fi was mulling, ignoring their banter.

"I remember seeing an Englishman in Kew wearing a long, thick coat on a hot summer day. I thought he was going to flash me so I called my neighbour out. My neighbour Steve is a tall African guy who looks as if he could beat up anybody and the long coated guy just turned and walked away." Fi's eyes gleamed

"I also had an English patient who came to his consultations without underpants so I'd have to look at his genitalia when I examined him. Wonder whether he'd qualify as a flasher?"

"Don't they like to be erect when they expose? If not erect it doesn't qualify."

"Certainly all the bridge players who want to expose themselves do. They even make comments telling me they are touching themselves when they talk to me on the telephone."

"Ugh" Yvan said "Do not tell me their names. It will spoil my concentration when I play with them. All I will be thinking of is what is under the edge of the bridge table"

Exhilaration fizzed in Fi's voice "I have to tell you about Dr Kayilasathanandan though because I'm interested in whether he did or did not flash. Let me know what you think. I was in Toronto at the time and that's why I know about it. Read it in the news. "

Yvan and Renee leant back in their chairs relaxed but exuding interest

Kayilasanathan's professional college claims he sexually abused a patient and committed disgraceful, dishonourable or unprofessional conduct — allegations that he denied. The patient's testimony formed the basis of the college's allegations against him otherwise he may still be practicing today.

The patient, identified only as Patient A due to a publication ban, was on the stand at Kayilasanathan's discipline proceedings at the College of Physicians and Surgeons of Ontario.

Tensions ran high in the hearing room because, for one thing, the patient whose testimony was highly anticipated did not even want to be there. She had tried unsuccessfully to quash a summons, which compelled her to testify. Had she refused, the college was prepared to enforce the summons and have the woman arrested and brought to the college.

"Oh my, they were out to get him"

Lawyers for the college and for Kayilasanathan frequently sparred over each other's line of questioning, jockeying for space at the podium to register objections in front of the five-member discipline panel, as the confused-looking witness was repeatedly asked to leave the room so the lawyers could make their arguments

"I essentially used him to get a (doctor's) note," the woman said under cross-examination by Kayilasanathan's lawyer. The doctor himself was not present Wednesday because it was a "full day" at the clinic where he worked

"How did they know of the case then to summon her?" Renee asked

"I'm getting to that Renee."

"She tells it like a story Renee. I love the build-up." Yvan said it softly but firmly

"The woman and Kayilasanathan met through mutual friends around 2003, and became reacquainted in late 2010,. The woman recounted a night of partying in Toronto with Kayilasanathan and a mutual friend, and an after-party at the condo of Kayilasanathan's brother, who was not home.

"We just started listening to music. I was drinking, all three of us were smoking weed," she said. The friend and Kayilasanathan were also doing cocaine, but she was not, she said."

"You doctors are disgraceful" Yvan said "I've never had cocaine"

"Neither have I" Fi retorted "But I guess it does happen. Lawyers I think are the biggest offenders.

"When did you read about it? Where?"

"In the "STAR". Dec.11th 2018. The day I arrived off the plane in Toronto. Great story"

Kayilsathananthan's witness said

"We were high. Hours go by. Next thing you know it's morning."

 The problem was the woman had an exam that Monday, for which she was not prepared due to the night out, she testified.

"We strategized about getting a doctor's note," she said under questioning. "I was in no position to take (the exam) after partying, so I was not prepared. He did mention he could get me a doctor's note. I said 'Sure, that would be great.'"

So she went to the Scarborough clinic where he worked on the Monday to get the note, she said. Although her medical chart from that day indicates a number of issues such as fever and chills, the patient admitted on the stand that none of that was actually discussed at the clinic. She was there strictly to get a note to get out of her exam, she testified. But she did have him examine her briefly with a stethoscope.

 "Because I said something like 'Shouldn't we make this look like a real doctor's visit?'" she testified.

"I'd strike him off for that" Yvan said" Fraudulent issue of sick notes"

 "Harmless I think Yvan. Lot's of sympathetic doctors give sick notes for no real reason but no one I know first gets intimate before writing a sick note and then personally pulls his penis out at a later date."

"How does she progress to a relationship that makes him think he can do so?" Renee asked

"They texted off and on that week; she had sensed that the doctor was being a bit flirtatious with her. She thought, 'Hey, he's a doctor, let me take a shot at him.'

"Attracted by the potential of big money?"

"I guess. They hooked up at a Mississauga hotel days later, she said. He was in no position to drive because he had been drinking, so she left in a cab. Kayilasanathan gave her some money for the fare, though it wasn't enough to cover the entire ride home."

"Cheap skate" Yvan looked disgusted. "He should at least pay for her ride home. He wanted free sex."

A few days later, the patient said, she was back at the clinic, very briefly, to get a second doctor's note to defer another exam, which the doctor gave her.

"I just thought it would be more believable at the college that it was the same doctor" writing a second note, she testified.

"So she was using him? Using her attractiveness?"

"That is not the concern of the Supervisory College Yvan. Only the doctor's behaviour is under their scrutiny."

The last time she saw him was when she visited his condo and he tried to make a move on her that she rejected.

"Why is she visiting him at his condo? Does she want more sick notes?"

"Poor bastard he is played along for what she can get out of him" He cast a shrewd look at Fi who nodded.

He eventually drove her home, exposing himself when they reached their destination.

"Weird. Was it vanity? Was the boner a humdinger?"

When she told the hearing about how his penis was exposed while sitting next to her in the front seat of the car, Dr. Kayilasanathan who was present asked her: "You sure?"

She was sure, she testified, saying she had already rebuffed his advances earlier that day at his condo. She. It was the last time she would see the Toronto doctor.

"This is my question to you both" Fi sounded exposed and curious as she spewed it out.

"If you have seen my goods before, why shouldn't I take them out again?" The words had hardly left her mouth when Yvan said

"What he wanted and what she wanted were completely different. Have you seen the British transport police analogy on 'you tube' Fi about consent? They use the cup of tea as the sexual analogy. It is explicit. You may have had 100 cups of tea with the same guy but on the 101st occasion if you don't want it you don't want it. You don't want to see his tea cup on this occasion" Yvan said it curtly, angry at Fi for not knowing something so basic

Fi laughed, not worried by Yvan's tightened mouth and expression "Good point Yvan. Yes I have seen the clip on 'You tube'. It is a very good analogy and a very clear explanation about consent."

"Did she report him for flashing? Was that how it came to light?" Renee asked

"No she didn't. She followed my train of thought about it being harmless in that context, or at least the process leading to exposure. She just ignored it proceeded to get out of her car and went into her house. When she went back to his clinic a month later, she saw another doctor, to whom she disclosed she had had sex with Kayilasanathan and that was what caused the problem"

"I have no intuition here Fi. So what happened?" Renee looked at her for a long moment trying to understand.

 "Renee, health care professionals are required by law in Ontario to report to their respective regulator if they know of other health care professionals and patients having sex."

The patient testified she never wanted to make a complaint about Kayilasanathan, had no ill will against him, and never wanted to be part of the discipline proceedings.

"As far as I'm concerned, my confidentiality, my privacy was breached," she said. "And I'm in this position now."

"His colleague didn't like him. Is that why he reported him?"

"Why did she tell the other doctor about it?" Renee was still looking confused

"I suppose she had to give an explanation of why she didn't want to see Kayilasanathan again and wanted someone else?"

"Is that the same in the UK?"Yvan asked

"Yes of course. Doctors are supposed to report inappropriate patient doctor relationships but I suspect one couple I know. Both bridge players. I think she was his patient but I can't prove it. I may be wrong. He was seeking women over several years before he hooked up with her."

"Bridge players who are doctors do not form a separate category Fi."

"True. There was another South African flasher doctor I heard about when I was playing at ACOL bridge club the other day. I'm trying to think of his name. It was in April 2014."

Yvan said "It must be pheromones causing these behaviours in these doctors otherwise why would they do it."

"Ah yes. I remember now. Dirk Redman. He qualified as a doctor in Cape Town, South Africa, in 2007. He now lives in Namibia. He exposed his erect penis to a nurse colleague in Sligo General Hospital in 2014. "

"Was his nice?" Renee said laughingly. Fi smiled.

"The following June, he exposes his penis and testicles to a 15-year-old girl in the same hospital where he had been working as a registrar in the emergency department.

Yvan said "How little one knows of the people one works with." Renee flashed back

"And what is under their trouser fronts" Fi undaunted said

"I think it was the age of the girl that really got the Medical Council fitness to practice committee upset; an under-age patient.   Redman was found guilty of disgraceful and dishonourable conduct which presented a serious risk. They cancelled his registration as a doctor. He must have appealed it because he was then struck off the medical register by the HIgh Court. "

"He exposed himself to a nurse and a teenage patient, in two separate incidents. What was his defence? "Yvan said this while getting up and standing behind his chair, pretending to be in the witness box.

"Me lud it was only on two occasions. And the patient looked older than 15. I didn't know she was a patient. I thought she had just accompanied someone to hospital. But what harm is there in showing it? I've got a nice looking one. Can I show it to you my luds and ladies" Yvan pretends to undo the zipper on his wool plaid trousers.

Fi burst out laughing at his posturing. "Why don't these flashers just take holidays in nudist colonies? They can show it off to whoever they please. They lose their livelihoods over a crazy sexual offence when they could go and live in that place in the south of France where you can even go supermarket shopping naked. He could comfortably practice as a doctor there and hide his erections behind the consulting desk."

"I know which one you mean. Cap d'Agde (**French** pronunciation: [kap dagd]) is the seaside resort in **France**.

The **Naturist Village** is a **town** by itself, with a 2 km (1 mi) beach, a large marina, 2,500 campsites and six restaurants bordering the **southern** end of the **nude** beach."

"But that is the point Fi. They want to show the erect gland. Which would you prefer to see?"

"Yours Yvan and now" Renee said

"Yvan. Need you ask? Neither flaccid ones nor erect ones; even if I do know the man. Interesting thought though. Is there a law in nudist colonies saying you can't show it erect? Surely not? Or maybe you wear a hat for the occasion and use it to cover the tent pole when it happens?" Fi was looking thoughtful

"I remember meeting up with a flasher when I was coming home from school. I was 15 years of age and for some unknown reason was standing at a bus stop waiting for my mother to pick me up. I remember it clearly to this day because she was unsympathetic when I told her about the flasher. I even remember his face and the size of his organ. There weren't many people around. I was the only one at the stop. I had my school uniform on and he was already at the stop when I walked towards it." Her voice was slightly unsteady

"He had already started playing with himself as it was big when I saw it. I felt a mixture of emotions. Disgust, sickness, fear, anxiety; not knowing what to do. I wasn't very brave then. I did have a boyfriend but I don't think I'd seen his erections."

"At fifteen?" Renee chirped "I saw my boyfriend's boner at age 13

"Asian girls are chaste Renee; especially the Catholic ones; Conscious of not offending God or being punished for doing so."

"Why was your mother unsympathetic?"

"She told me I should have taken my 12inch ruler out and…

"Measured it? " Yvan was laughing

Fi got angry. "No she wanted me to hit it over and over again. Later she apologised to me and said that she had a similar distressing event when she was a young girl and wished she had taken her ruler out and hit it. Her feelings and words were driven by her anger at not having prepared me for the situation. If I had behaved like that, her hatred and anger from her childhood would have been vanquished; vindicated 30 years later."

Renee and Yvan had both fallen silent. They could see Fi's hurt in her darkened eyes

"Sorry I lost my temper" she said "I get upset every time I think of it."

Yvan tried to lighten the heaviness that had descended "Back to the nudist colony. Are children not allowed to come into them? Does this automatically disqualify interest from paedophiles?"

"Questions, questions, questions" Rene said. "Tell me tomorrow. After doing so badly in this evening's game of bridge and Fi's revelations I can't concentrate on this interesting chit chat."

Fi pretended a cooler than cool persona to hide her emotions as she said to Yvan

"Come on my lovely Dorogoy, we must go. I'm tired and drained of energy. Coming third tonight wasn't too bad but all that intense concentration followed by re-living my childhood has just made me want to cuddle up in the silk satin sheets next to your warm body."

3.   **THE PAEDOPHILE**

They returned home. It was the weekend and his maid was off duty. Fi preferred to be with Yvan when he was on his own as she felt more comfortable without "the hired hand" around. They had developed a routine of playing the Friday evening bridge game and Fi staying over for the weekend. She always left on Sunday night.

"She knows you have been here Fi. She has to make up your bed."

"I felt odd the other day when she came in and I was having breakfast with you."

"You should have. That night you slept in my bed and your bed wasn't messed up so she knew. I'm surprised she didn't get the ultraviolet light out and try to distinguish whether there were female secretions in my bed."

"I kept my panties on all night Yvan." Fi said it softly yet defensively

"Sometimes I wonder whether when she arranges my things whether she looks for evidence of sexuality, video's with adult content Fi ; that sort of thing. She has a sly complacent smile some days as if she knows what I do."

"That's how they discovered the only paedophile haematologist that I knew of." Fi said

"You worked with one?"

"No. When I went to work at Addenbrookes Hospital Cambridge he had already been jailed. It was sad because everyone told me about it. They were ashamed and disgusted and remorseful that they hadn't recognised his sick soul."

Saturday morning was always leisurely. Fi was curled up under a blanket still wearing Yvan's pyjamas. The burgundy contrasted strongly with his cream leather sofa. The room was a masculine room lightened by the pale Italian Natuzzi furniture. Yvan put down the newspaper he had been half scanning while he had been talking to her. He took his black rimmed glasses off and said

"Tell me all" He sat back in his leather arm chair, his smoking jacket pulled around him and said "The only reason I am with you, despite you never having sex with me is because you make life interesting." Fi gave a wry smile. "I do have sex with you. It's just not penetrative."

"That's probably what the paedophiles who don't have penetrative sex say." He held out his hand in an encouraging gesture asking her to carry on.

"For his patients and their parents Myles Bradbury was a "God-like" figure. In reality, he was a paedophile who secretly filmed his abuse of patients."

"How did he get away with it? Surely someone accompanies children?" Yvan looked away from her at the autumn dawn breaking over the River Thames as if to distract himself from his inward images of Myles.

"Why wasn't he caught at the first attempt?"

In July 2012, the UK's Child Exploitation and Online Protection Centre (CEOP) - which is meant to protect against child abuse - received a list of 2,235 names.

It was sent by police in Canada following a raid on the headquarters of Avoz Films, a website selling what it referred to as "just legal" and "naturist" films.

Myles Bradbury, a paediatric consultant at Addenbrooke's Hospital in Cambridge, was on that list because he had bought a film from them while working in Birmingham in 2005.

CEOP - which Toronto Police say were once leaders in the field - took no action for 16 months against Bradbury - who went on to admit 25 sex offences against patients and making thousands of indecent images of children from the internet.

"That is bizarre. Were the police part of the ring of paedophiles? Bloody useless as cops if not."

They only started investigating when the Canadians announced they were going public about their investigation, named Project Spade. That no action was taken in the UK for more than a year has stunned police in Toronto. Despite repeated calls from Toronto to London to find out what was happening they did nothing allowing Myles to continue his abuse.

Detective Sgt Kim Gross, who is in charge of the child exploitation team in Toronto, claims CEOP - which now comes under the National Crime Agency (NCA) - "dropped the ball".

"The f..king British are useless" Yvan said "If I had failed that badly I would walk away from the work and have someone replace me."

Fi looked at Yvan in surprise. She said "Those are the very words used by Detective Sergeant Kim Gross to the BBC Inside Out East.

"Everyone will think that; unless of course they were in the paedophile ring."

"Yet between July 2012 and November 2013, Bradbury was free to carry on abusing cancer patients - sometimes while their parents sat in ignorance on the other side of a hospital curtain."

"They should have got material from a follow up source at least. Not just do nothing"

On the same day that Suffolk Police were finally informed, via West Midlands Police, about Bradbury, Addenbrooke's Hospital suspended the doctor following a family complaint about an intimate examination of a child.

"So the police still did nothing until a family member complained"

"Yes and no one has asked the question why? My presumed answer is because there was high level involvement in Cambridge with loads of other people doing the same thing and part of the ring. Probably politicians and leaders involved." Yvan studied her countenance trying to get to the bottom of the why's and wherefore's of the lack of investigation.

"Bradbury's wife was pregnant at the time." The intense look Yvan threw at her when Fi said this caused her to shiver.

"Was it their first child?"

"Don't know." Fi knew what Yvan was thinking. 'Was he abusing his own children?'

 "Any other paedophiles in the vicinity who formed part of the ring?"

"The Bradbury's lived in Herringswell, Suffolk and no one came forward. The Suffolk Police's investigation into Bradbury, revealed the devious steps he had taken to cover his tracks."

"That may be the alternative explanation Fi of why it took so long to discover and arrest him"

"I don't think so. I think the police were part of the network and that's why they failed to do justice."

One of the little boys who he had used for his perverted activities said this. Fi mimicking a little boy accent said

 "He always wanted me on my own. And then he'd want to check me. Instead of checking just my joints, he'd want to check my whole body. He'd make me strip down. He focussed on my private parts."

"You have just ruined my Saturday morning" Yvan said "How mentally sick is that pervert"

"What is frightening about the story is that the British police did not investigate Myles for 18 months allowing him to continue offending. When I was working in Cambridge I thought there were lots of sexually queer people out there. I think the police were probably part of a cartel of paedophiles or the sex rings. I just sensed it was an odd environment. Probably senior politicians involved as well."

4.   THE VOYEUR

Fi slept in her own room that Saturday night. She had wanted an undisturbed night and had been gentle but firm in her rejection. She was exhausted and didn't want Yvan tossing and turning beside her. The next morning Yvan came into her room looking at her with those sleepy dangerous eyes that had first attracted Fi. He pulled back the curtain slightly and peered out. He gasped

"She's doing it again. She takes her clothes off with the curtains wide open. I think she wants me to look at her.

Fi's voice emerged sleepily from the bed "Don't be silly Yvan she doesn't know that you are behind the curtains peering out at her. Who is she? How old?"

"It is my neighbour's adolescent daughter."

"She probably doesn't think you are an old voyeuristic pervert. You look harmless enough." Yvan turned away immediately at Fi's words

"I was just checking on the day."

"Jump into bed and keep warm. I'll tell you about a voyeuristic pervert I knew who lost a fortune from his sexuality." Rested and refreshed she welcomed him and tried to make amends for rejecting him the night before. Her perspicacity was spot on.

Yvan crossed over to her, took off his silk dressing gown and crawled slowly in beside her naked. He felt a sense of belonging as he experienced her warmth. Daringly, he put his hand out and placed it on her breast.

Fi turned so his hand was dislodged and said "Wait till I've finished my story otherwise you will distract me"

"I want to distract you."

"Not now. I worked with the voyeur at the Royal Berkshire Hospital in Reading. I thought he was a lovely guy. He looked harmless. I co-authored a scientific paper with him although I remember writing all of it.

"That sounds like fraud to me."

"Sounds like it to me too but it was standard practice. A non-medic at the Hammersmith Hospital had his name on all the scientific papers. He had a foreign name Richard Sydzlo . Photographer or statistician or something like that.

"What about your man? The fortune losing voyeur?

"He earned himself a Wikipedia page Yvan. That's the way to get fame."

"Notoriety you mean"

"Jonathan Mark Fielden was relatively young when he lost his fortune His first consultant post was at Royal Berkshire NHS Foundation Trust, Reading, in anaesthesia and intensive care medicine. That was where I met him. He was born on 9 September 1963 which I know, because the hospital celebrated his 40th birthday with a party in the Consultant's lounge and I did a song and dance act at it."

"You remember some weird things about people"

"Jonathon rose like a star in the firmament. He went from Reading, which is a hospital of no fame whatsoever, to become the medical director of University College London Hospitals NHS Foundation Trust. He was chairman from 2006 to 2009 of the Central Consultants and Specialists Committee of the British Medical Association, and served as the secondary care specialist on the governing body of Aylesbury Vale Clinical Commissioning Group. From this he became Director of Specialised Commissioning for NHS England. This and his Medical directorship of University College Hospital meant he was a mega-massive top dog."

"That's boring to know Fi. So he has a glittering career and is rising to senior positions but where's the sex bit?"

"I'm building up to that Yvan. I just wanted to let you know how everybody along the way was fooled, me included. Jonathon was a stupid idiot"

"Not interested. Want to know about the voyeur side."

"I am not exactly sure about the details but I think he owned a separate house which he was renting out to guests away from his home. He spied on a 15-year-old through a hole in a bathroom ceiling and she noticed."

"She sensed something and perceived his devilish gaze?"

"Yup. After realising someone was watching her take a shower, the teenager was traumatised. She had been left so deeply shocked that, for a number of months she couldn't bring herself to take showers."

"But surely bathroom ceilings have no holes?"

"There was a hole in the light fixture in the ceiling and a ventilation shaft. Jonathon was in the loft directly above the shower. He looked down the ventilation pipe to watch her shower obviously for his own sexual gratification."

"Imagine looking up while you are showering and seeing an eye in the ceiling spying on you. He must have known he was rumbled when they made eye contact"

"The teenager eventually told other members of her family what had happened and, the mother discussed it with the girl's school counsellor who reported it to the police. Jon was arrested in December 2016."

Yvan sighed. "Cretin"

"He said to the police that he had watched the teenager for 15 to 20 seconds."

"It is not that he watched accidentally but that it was a deliberate set-up to allow him to watch Fi."

"At the hearing his defending barrister Alexandra Felix tried to make excuses about the amount of time he watched her. She said "He accepts it shouldn't have happened, but it did, but not because of any concerted effort to do it. Circumstances arose for it to happen.""

"Are they trying to say he hadn't set it up deliberately?"

"Yes. Any excuse would do"

The barrister said Fielden had a high pressure job and had been under "particular stresses" which caused a "loss of judgment."

"Well I don't buy the "high pressure job" excuse. Was it one event?"

"Yvan I despair of you sometimes. Who has a ventilation hole through which you can see into a bathroom? A guaranteed place to see people naked? Of course it wasn't one event. It was probably the first time he was discovered."

Yvan gave a 'C'est la vie' gesture.

"Actually I do know someone who did do something similar to that. It reminds me of a Sri Lankan doctor I know. Female this time. She built an apartment in her house and the bathroom of the apartment had a shared window into her bedroom. She explained to me that she had a curtain over it from her side but I bet she spied on people from her side. She was an anaesthetist as well.

"Are all anaesthetists perverted like Jon?"

"They are looking at naked unconscious bodies all the time so I do not understand why they should want to spy on living, breathing, walking ones? What is the fascination? Jonathon certainly was a pervert."

"Just one incident Fi"

"Only one reported. The court was told that following Jonathon's arrest his mobile phone was examined. The websites he had visited featured underage girls and child sex abuse images."

One of Yvan's legs lodged between Fi's thighs opening them up"

"No possibility Yvan" Fi said to him bring her legs together and continuing her story. "Despite this evidence Jon's barrister tried to defend these images as well. ;He accepts he hit upon them while looking at adult pornography.'

"Absolute poppycock" Yvan said. "You know that pornographic double- pronged guys video that Steve sent round? I deleted it straight away. I didn't store it. It made me sick."

"Unfortunately I think your phone stores it forever. I haven't checked but I think it does. The only way to get rid of it is to throw the phone into a river; a deep one. Then it won't come to light"

"You can examine my phone. I won't be throwing it away"

"I need to investigate why Jonathon chose this voyeuristic path. He had a privileged background, had been privately-educated at Bedford School before going to Bristol University and went on from the dungeons of Reading to have a glittering career so why do this?".

After Jonathon's arrest on a suspicion of voyeurism, he was suspended from working by the General Medical Council a month later.

"How does that happen?   How was it actioned so quickly?"

"If a doctor is arrested by the police, they report it to the General Medical Council straight away and the GMC weigh up the offence and suspend him rapidly if it is serious enough"

"Sounds like it was his own home."

"Not sure. The newspaper says he was convicted of voyeurism against a child which took place at a private address in Leighton Buzzard which I think he must have owned separate from his family home."

"In June 2019 he was given a suspended sentence and was eventually erased from the register - "struck off" - by the Medical Practitioner Tribunal Service in January 2020. They did not like voyeurism against a child."

"Why did they take so long? Dec 2016 to January 2020?"

"I have no idea. He must have appealed the process and of course with his salary he would have continued to be paid till he was finally found guilty."

Yvan was still pursuing Fi's body. His right hand searching and opening the possibility of something reckless. Soft sure movements, slowly and then faster

"Yvan" she said her conversation stopped, racked by shivers of pleasure. He sucked on the skin of her throat and continued downwards his hand never stopping till he felt her release. Fire shot through her core. She said "Penetrative sex will be boring after this"

Yvan moving as quickly as he could mounted Fi and within a few rapid movements released himself between her thighs which were gripping him firmly. She heard him giving a low moan of delight as he shuddered. 'Who invented inter-labial intercourse?' he thought. 'Almost as good as the real thing'

He slid off her and said half dozily "You go first. I'll shower next."

Yvan's phone rang, awakening him from his post-emission state. He had a brief conversation with his asset manager. Fi could hear them talking as she showered.

 When she appeared Yvan stopped studying his mobile phone which detailed his colossal fortune. The asset manager had e-mailed it to him with the most recent trades that he had done. He stared at Fi who emerged from the bathroom having got rid of his smell and the secretions on her thighs. She was smiling

"Maria is going to know what you've done Yvan. It's splattered in the bed"

"Ahh who cares. It's obviously something that I've thought about but I am not going to dwell too much on the housemaid's view of the soiled bed-sheets. What happened to Jonathon?"

"You are wide awake for someone who has just ejaculated."

"Just checked some trading today. I have made a million on the markets."

"Don't lose it all as Jonathon did. Although Jon may still be very rich as he is on a mega-massive pension now. When he resigned from the NHS commissioning group for England, guess what he was earning?"

"One hundred k? One fifty thousand?"

"At the time of his arrest at age 55 he was on a salary of £224,999 a year, making him one of the highest paid doctors in the country."

A shocked chortle emerged from Yvan "Three times an idiot. Mission impossible to ever regain that sum after what he did" He pursed his lips. "What does this guy look like? I'm curious to know what a real idiot looks like."

"Remind me to show you a picture of myself with him. I got someone to take it at a charity event we both were attending."

"Did he go to jail?"

"No; being high powered means you get off lightly in the UK."

Judge Foster sentenced Jonathon to five months imprisonment, which he suspended for 12 months. He ordered Jon to carry out 150 hours of unpaid work, pay costs of £3,500 and attend 30 Rehabilitation Activity Requirement days. He was made the subject of a sexual harm prevention order and his name is on the sex Offenders' register.

"Ironic; a light punishment."

"Yes he got away scot free. Lots of money from his pension, no jail sentence and his name on a sex offenders register. Do you know why?"

Yvan's long sunburned fingers were clutching the white sheets trying to control his amazement at the easy life Jonathon had, even after paedophilic offending.

"People who apologise, say they are sorry and appear humble before a judge always get a lighter sentence."

"Tell me more about him at breakfast. I'm going to shower and you can come in and watch. I'll put on a show for you and you can call your anaesthetist friend. She is welcome. She doesn't need to spy from behind her curtains in her bedroom.

"She lives a long way from here so won't be able to get to you in a hurry Yvan." Fi was laughing "Maybe I'll suggest it to her another day?"

"I'll read you what Google says over breakfast about Jon. I'm going to sleep now in my own bed. You can sleep with your emissions.

"That is my bed too Fi. I'm coming in it."

"You've already 'come' in yours Yvan. I do not wish you to come in mine" They both laughed as Yvan headed towards the shower.

When he returned Fi was asleep. He looked down at her hair and body and felt a wave of love. He thought 'I almost believe in God when I see you, here in my bed Fi'

He slid in beside her. He remembered her shyness and hang-ups when they had first started becoming more intimate. They were a distant relic of their past. He turned on the light on the bedside table. Fi had never liked him looking at her but he loved the contrast of their bodies. He loved seeing his pale skin against her tanned flesh. After feasting his eyes on her naked body he switched off the lamp leaving the glow from the chandelier in the hallway to bathe them through the partly closed door

Fi read out Jon's Wikipedia page to Yvan at breakfast.

 Jonathon married Christine Mundin, head of media at the British Medical Association in 2010 and divorced in 2019

"She didn't want to stay with him Fi."

He had chaired the CQC team which assessed Hinchingbrooke Hospital run by Circle Health Ltd (the first privately managed NHS hospital) as "inadequate" He was appointed director of specialised commissioning at NHS England in October 2015. Subsequently, he was reckoned by the Health Service Journal to be the 49th most influential person in the English NHS in 2015.

"Brains in his bollocks; trading all that for a spying activity." Yvan's features shouted derision. "Did you hear the joke about the little boy in the bath?"

"No. Tell me"

"The little boy looks down at his testicles when he is bathing. He asks his mum 'Are these my brains?'

The mum replies. "No but they soon will be"

After tootles of laughter from Fi and their breakfast completed, Yvan looked at Fi curiosity in his voice "Tell me more about voyeurs and paedophiles. Are they interlinked?"

"I guess if you are not harming anyone and just looking at images you can be a doctor because no one knows your thoughts but the question is at what point do you put your thoughts into practice?"

"After reading about all these reprehensible creeps who are looking after patients I wish they would invent something that would help you identify what people think when they look at naked bodies."

"Does it matter what you think so long as you act professionally?"

"And don't act irregularly?"

"Paedophiles who don't act on their thoughts and the images they view think that it is ok"

"Don't they all?"

"No. There is a group who call themselves 'Virtuous paedophiles'"

5   THE VIRTUOUS PAEDOPHILE

"People make excuses for their own behaviour" Yvan said "How can you be virtuous and a paedophile?"

"They are paedophilic in their own heads. They never practice hands on sex. There was a good article in the New York times about it. 'Emerging psychology of paedophiles'

"Give me the gist of it"

"No no I'll read out the relevant parts to you"

The relationship between viewing or collecting images and committing hands-on abuse is a matter of continuing debate among some experts, and one that is critical to evaluating the risk an offender poses. Until recently, the prevailing view was that only a minority of people caught viewing such images, between 5 and 20 percent, also committed physical abuse.

That perception began to change in 2007, when a pair of psychologists at the Federal Bureau of Prisons reported that 85% of convicted online offenders acknowledged in therapy that they had raped or otherwise sexually abused children.

That finding circulated widely before the study was formally published, created an uproar among therapists, researchers and law enforcement specialists. The prisons bureau balked at publishing it at all, and withdrew it from a peer-reviewed journal close to its release date.

Many cited concerns that the study sample was biased: It was based on the confessions of 155 convicts who had sought out therapy in prison, not on a representative sample of paedophiles, a much broader group with diverse habits.

"It was what we call a convenience sample — that was a legitimate criticism," said Michael L. Bourke, co-author of the study with Andres E. Hernandez. Dr. Bourke is now chief of the behavioural analysis unit of the United States Marshals.

Since then, several other studies have supported the prison finding, if not precisely the 85% number. In one, inspectors from an array of government agencies interviewed 127 online offenders shortly after their arrests. Less than 5% admitted to previously molesting at least one child.

When agents followed up with more in-depth, polygraph-assisted methods, another 53% admitted to hands-on offenses, a total of nearly 60%.

"This was not a convenience sample; these were offenders, some of whom had downloaded just a single image, with no known history, from all over the country, interviewed by people from different agencies," Dr. Bourke said. "They had zero incentive to admit to a previous offense — very much the opposite."

The high rate of previous, hands-on offending undermines another common assumption about paedophiles. "We shouldn't assume that viewing online images leads to abuse of a child victim in person," said Joe Sullivan, a specialist in sex crimes against children in Ireland and Britain. "In my clinical experience, it's the other way around. Most of these men have already committed hands-on offenses."

From this point of view, downloading abuse images — and especially connecting with groups of like-minded paedophiles online — does not awaken latent desires. The desires are very much awake and, in many cases, have already been acted on. But the images and online communities can help erode inhibitions further, drawing paedophiles into more frequent or more aggressive acts, Dr. Bourke said.

"What you see, in their search histories," he said, "is that they learn how to evade law enforcement, they become more confident and they begin to use cognitive distortions to overcome their moral inhibitions."

Some therapists and researchers say these findings from law enforcement threaten to unfairly tar people who never act on their desires. This group certainly exists — they're sometimes called "virtuous paedophiles" — but in an era of increasing alarm over the proliferation of online abuse, they are going only further.

"Are paedophiles born or made?"Yvan questioned

"Some people think that everything is environmental but I've always supported the view especially for cancer that it is genes and the environment interacting."

Yvan's emotions thickened his words. "My dad died of pancreatic cancer but he loved Russian vodka so you may be correct Fi."

"It's exemplified in breast cancer where you may carry the genes but without the environment i.e. a breast you don't get breast cancer."

"Do paedophiles carry genes for paedophilia? What drives people to sexually abuse children?"

"There are lots of theories on the aetiology. I'll read out what the New York Times says

"The biological clues attached to paedophilia demonstrate that its roots are prenatal," said James Cantor, director of the Toronto Sexuality Centre. "These are not genetic; they can be traced to specific periods of development in the womb."

Psychological and environmental factors may also contribute, though it is not yet clear what those are or how they interact with developmental conditions.

By contrast, the common presumption that paedophiles were themselves abused as children now has less support. Child victims are at far greater risk of future substance abuse, depression, persistent traumatic stress or criminal aggression than of becoming molesters. The vast majority of offenders deny any sex abuse in their childhood, even though they could garner sympathy in court by doing so, experts say. "A chaotic childhood increases the likelihood of a chaotic adulthood, of any kind," Dr. Cantor said.

"My childhood in the war was chaotic Fi"

"I feel for you. Now I know why I'm so straight and virtuous Yvan. I had an ordered childhood. We said the rosary every evening on our knees. We sat at our study desks after dinner, and in the mornings, when on holiday. Irrespective of what we did at those desks we had to sit there. I remember my sister Melanie had comic books in her desk whereas I studied. She became a music teacher and I, a doctor."

"Ha ha love the comic books. The paedophiles? What makes them?"

"Science, in recent years has begun to provide some answers. One thing most paedophiles have in common: They discover, usually as teenagers, that their sexual preferences have not matured like everyone else's. Most get stuck on the same-age boys or girls who first attracted them at the start of puberty, though some retain interest in far younger children."

"People don't choose what arouses them — they discover it," said Dr. Fred Berlin, director of the Johns Hopkins Sex and Gender Clinic. "No one grows up wanting to be a paedophile."

"Nabokov's Lolita?"

"Yes. His male character didn't achieve sexual maturity so he fixated on Lolita who was adolescent not extremely under age."

"I don't believe they are virtuous" Yvan said "They will offend

"There was a surgeon at Stoke where I worked who never abused, just looked. He was a non-hands-on paedophile. I prefer that term. Paedophiles are not virtuous."

Cristian Bogdan, 43, a heart and lung NHS surgeon was caught with nearly 40,000 images and videos of child pornography that featured children as young as four. The paedophile, who is a married father-of-one from Congleton in Cheshire, claimed he had been 'stressed' while working at Royal Stoke University Hospital.

"See the excuse? Stress leads me to behave in this perverted way. They shouldn't bother to make excuses. Their behaviour is indefensible."

Detectives raided his home and found the pornography across 33 different electronic devices.

"Thirty three?" his eyebrows arched upward

"Yes. I wish I knew what they were?"

"Was he trying to cover his disturbing tracks by using this number of devices? I presume they did mean devices not just memory sticks or CD's"

"He probably planned his life with some way of evading; hence all the devices. That is my theory."

"Did the raid occur while you were working at Stoke?"

"No long after. The raid occurred on December 1, 2017, after a tip-off. Officers from Cheshire Police's Paedophile and Cyber Investigation team discovered indecent images of children aged between four and six while other pictures were of youngsters aged six to eight. The films involved a girl aged 14."

"Did he even bother to protest his innocence?"

"Bogdan initially made no comment following his arrest but later handed himself in at Macclesfield Police Station in January 2019 and handed over a prepared statement.

In it he stated he became 'interested' in file sharing and downloading peer to peer software to his computer in 2015. He then started downloading sexual images, but he stated that the vast majority of the images he downloaded were 'family or non-prohibited images.'"

"Yeah and the child porn appears by accident? How can he possibly defend it?"

"At Chester Crown Court he pleaded guilty to three charges of making indecent photographs of children, one of possessing indecent photographs of children and one count of possessing prohibited images of children."

"Was he jailed?"

"He was struck off; banned from working. Ordered to complete 150 hours of unpaid work and made subject to a Sexual Harm Prevention Order for 10 years.

"That takes us to 2029 when he will probably reoffend."

At the time Judge Steven Everett told him: 'It is really important to get across to you, and people like you, that these are not just images but real people, they involve young children who have been sexually abused."

"So the Judge didn't buy the story of the virtuous paedophile who was stressed at work?"

"No. The judge said 'Whatever you were doing at the time, you must have realised what you did. The stress of being a consultant may be part of it, but that is no excuse. You showed you are not fit to be a doctor. No-one can trust you with any person, let alone a child. You should never be allowed near patients again.'

"That sounds absolutely correct" Yvan eyes were steely, his face grim when he said this.

At the tribunal hearing the lawyer appearing for the General Medical Council, said: 'The judge set out certain mitigation features in relation to the doctor in that he appeared to be remorseful and the fact he had apparently a loyal and supportive wife and a family and that he was working with the Lucy Faithful foundation.

"What's that?"

"Lucy Faithfull, Baroness Faithfull was a British social worker and children's campaigner who was born in South Africa. She founded the Lucy Faithfull Foundation, the only nation-wide UK child protection charity working to prevent child sexual abuse."

Bogdan gave no reason for not attending the disciplinary hearing. During his court case, his lawyer Peter Wright QC said: 'He is of previous good character with a distinguished medical career that is now utterly destroyed.

'He has been ostracised professionally, socially shamed, and is ashamed by his conduct. But he does not want to minimise or excuse that conduct - his downfall is his own making. The people pictured are the victims and he realises that, and he is determined to correct this as much as he can.'

Dr John Oxtoby, Royal Stoke's medical director, said: 'Mr Bogdan was a surgeon whose work involved the care of adults and he had no contact with children. There are no reasons for patients to be concerned."

"Do they acccept that the heart, the soul of their body is being repaired by a pervert? What a bloody stupid idiot he was. At work he holds down a difficult and respected job but at home he is searching for and downloading thousands of images of children being sexually abused."

"In interview he tried to downplay the amount of images he had, claiming he'd downloaded them in bulk and deleted most of them but it was clear that he was continually actively seeking out these dreadful images of abuse. He had no previous convictions and held a well-paid responsible job yet he risked all of that in the pursuit of these crimes."

"Sexual abuse has a dreadful impact on victims and the sexual abuse of children can have long lasting effects for the rest of their lives. He should go to jail" Yvan looked serious.

"Ones childhood determines the events of one's future lives. But just because they don't practice hands-on don't they know that looking at these images increases market forces for more images to be sourced by distributors of child pornography?"

"Let me look it up Yvan" His smile had given way to puckered lines that seemed to have frozen on his cheeks. He arose and peered over Fi's shoulder as she read the article on her laptop. His right hand massaged her neck slowly working sensuously on the upper part of her spine.

"What is paedophilia? In Asian countries don't they marry 12-year olds off to their rich 35 year old Uncles? Is it just cultural? The Greeks always had young boys servicing them."

"There is a definition here in this article."

"Preying on Children: The Emerging Psychology of Paedophiles by Benedict Carey"

 Over the past generation, psychologists, forensic specialists and others have studied paedophilia, a disorder characterized by "recurrent, intense arousing fantasies, urges or behaviours involving sexual activity with a prepubescent child," according to psychiatry's diagnostic manual.

Some therapists and researchers say these findings from law enforcement threaten to unfairly tar people who never act on their desires. This group certainly exists — they're sometimes called "virtuous paedophiles" — but in an era of increasing alarm over the proliferation of online abuse, they are going only further underground.

"That is a shame, a tragedy," Dr. Cantor said. "That is the group we need to learn about. That's the kind of person we'd like our clients to become, a person who's aware of the urges and learns to effectively manage them."

Learning to manage a drive as visceral, and often consuming, as sexual desire, is possible, therapists say, but it cannot be shut off; nor can it be replaced, the way heroin can be swapped for methadone. Treatment can require drugs that reduce circulating testosterone and software that limits online browsing habits.

Often, therapy addresses substance abuse as well. Studies suggest that at least 40% of sex offenders were using drugs or alcohol when they committed their crimes.

"The important thing, I think, is that people know that treatment is possible," Dr. Berlin said. "There's a subgroup out there, they refer themselves here, and they are quite convinced that they do not want real-life sex with children."

"Not good enough for me" Yvan said. "Isn't there something in your bible about the thought is the same as the deed?"

Fi was impressed. "You are quoting the bible to me? I thought you were a non-believer?"

"There is good in all religious books, the Torah, Bible, Quran and anything else you like to look at. I'd like to extend your mother's treatment to them. Hit it hard with a ruler if ever it rises looking at a child. That should prevent them from looking. Is there anything known about this kind of behaviour-dissuading therapy?"

"Hmm I need to look that up. I wonder whether they have tried any kind of Antabuse-type treatment?"

"What's that?"

"Alcoholics are given a substance- Antabuse which makes them feel ill every time they drink alcohol. Eventually they associate alcohol consumption with feeling ill and don't want to drink anymore."

"That sounds like a good method of treatment for alcoholism I'd recommend 'Mama's ruler treatment' for paedophiles and voyeurs.'

"Haha Yvan. I'm crazy about you. I think you are gorgeous and sooo funny. Good treatment. Mama's ruler treatment"

Yvan smiled. A wave of desire washed over him as his eyes met Fi's. She had turned to look at him. He averted his gaze to avoid the expected, below-waist reaction. "Does paedophilia go with a particular medical speciality?"

"There are probably more paedophiles in paediatrics. They choose the speciality to be close to their targets. Any speciality though, methinks."

Yvan said "On that rationale why are gynaecologists, gynaecologists? Because they get to look at millions of different women spreading their legs for them?"

"I have one friend who did gynaecology. I'll ask him. Meanwhile here's another non paediatric perv caught in a rather unusual way."

"In a childrens bookshop?"

"No but I am convinced that a guy who was alone in Richmond theatre where there were loads of children in a children's play was a paedophile. He stood out so conspicuously."

"So who was the paediatric perv caught unusually?"

"Dr Adrian Marsden, an NHS psychiatrist addicted to child abuse images was found out when an amateur dramatics coach helped him download a mobile phone app to learn his lines."

Charmaine Parkin, the coach was shocked to find a thumbnail of a vile image of a child and confronted the psychiatrist. Police later found almost 2,000 sickening images on his computer after this came to light.

"She reported him?"

"Yes. Marsden, who worked at an NHS adolescent mental health treatment centre, admitted he had a 'fetish' for child abuse images and viewed it to help him ease stress."

"Yeah sure" Yvan said sarcastically

"One of these occasions when he was viewing these images was after the 2017 inquest of tragic teenager Becky Romero.

Dr. Marsden was 60 at the time, a married father-of-two. Becky Romero's parents were apoplectic after he decided to discharge the 15-year-old who tragically hanged herself days later.

"I wonder whether he abused Becky?"

"That was my thought too Yvan. Maybe that led to her killing herself?"

"In the hearing they said that 'Dr Marsden separated his professional and private life and never acted upon his urges through contact with children but how would they know? Children often don't say anything."

Becky's mother Nicky Romero expressed her disgust that he didn't get jail time after being convicted of possessing child abuse images. She said: 'He worked in an adolescent unit where he took children into a little room to talk one-to-one with them. Yet he was behaving like this? I am gobsmacked.

'I have been through so much stress because of what happened but I dealt with it. Most people who are stressed go for a walk or have a drink, they don't turn to that.;

"It seems to be a stock excuse" Yvan said "Oh I'm stressed so I'll look at paedophilic images, or be a voyeur or whatever else that gets my pecker up."

 Becky's mum said 'I wish he had gone to jail and am disgusted that he hasn't. He has got away with it scot-free.'

"I support what she said" Yvan said "When you are doing that kind of thing and a child is in front of you how can you be concentrating on your job? Or looking at the child in a non-sexual way?"

'He decided to be heavily engaged in Sex Addicts Anonymous after the hearing as he was struck off by the General Medical Council.

'He retired before he could be struck off. His wife and family are strangely standing by him.'

"I'm afraid they shouldn't Yvan. Although if I discovered you were a paedophile I'm not sure what I would do."

"Have my passwords to my computer and phone you Babushka. You won't find a thing on them."

Marsden pleaded guilty to making indecent photos of children and possessing prohibited images of children under the Protection of Child Act (1978) at Poole Magistrates' Court.

He avoided jail and was instead fined £2,500 and given a five year Sexual Harm Prevention Order, an 18 month community order and told to pay £85 costs and an £85 victim surcharge.

"Some people get jail sentences and I'm not sure how they make the distinction of who to send to jail."

"The severity of the offence? Hand-on offending?"

"Maybe. Dr Jonathan Walsh was jailed. He was aged 47 when he was sentenced. He was a married father-of-two when he downloaded at least 27 abuse films from the internet during his time off from treating sick children. He says he distributed child porn because he was 'tired of his job'.

"What a lame excuse. Why even bother to make it"

The paediatric consultant published 24 of these on a secret website where paedophiles swap graphic images with each other.

The films featured boys and girls aged two to eight and had a total playing time of 18 hours. All but one, were classed as Category A images – meaning they showed the most serious type of abuse. During a police raid on his home in September 2015 detectives believe he may have downloaded many more child porn films, as they found 300 files had been deleted from his computer.

He was jailed for three years unlike the paedophile doctor who worked at Great Ormond Street Hospital (GOSH), Ralph Harper, who at age 31 and as a junior doctor, downloaded dozens of videos showing children as young as eight being raped and sexually abused. Harper worked as a junior doctor at GOSH from September 2016 to March 2017, then moved to the neonatal department at London's St Mary's hospital

"Where Will and Kate had their royal babies delivered?"

"Yes. Prosecutors said it was "particularly worrying" that he committed the offences while working with ill and vulnerable children as a junior doctor.

"The images found on Harper's personal laptop were of children aged between eight and 14 years old, and included 21 category A moving images – the most serious kind,"

"What is that? Moving images?"

"Videos. Like the ones Steve sends round""

"Harper, I think will now accept the consequences of his actions in regards to future employment in the medical profession. He should not practice again"

"Yes. He was put on the sex offenders' register and handed a sexual harm prevention order."

"Downloading illegal images of children I think deserves a jail sentence" Yvan said. "He chose to be a junior doctor in the paediatric sphere, so his conduct was particularly worrying as he intended to commit crime."

"He too like Marsden the psychiatrist was spared an immediate prison sentence over the indecent images of children."

"The children may have been too young to tell if Ralph Harper had sexually assaulted them" Yvan said. "The bastard should go to jail. They are too bloody lenient on these perverts. How can they allow it?"

"Two reasons I think, One, he is apologetic before the judge and demonstrates insight into his offending, and two,   because senior police officers call for the government to consider "alternatives" to prosecution to ease immense strain on the criminal justice system. That's why they get away scot free."

"Mama's ruler treatment, five times a day at home is what I'd give them" Yvan said "with a sharp edge to the ruler that causes bleeding."

 Fi said "That is lacking in understanding Yvan. Don't be appalling" Fi wound her arms round his neck to soften the harshness of her words.

"Scientists seek to understand how the disorder develops. There is growing consensus that the origin is largely biological. This view is based in part on studies pointing to subtle physical traits that have a higher incidence among paedophiles.

"Yes I've seen that. The smile of the paedophile"

Fi was nodding. "These findings also defy common stereotypes about what paedophilia is. The majority of convicted offenders are men who prey on children ages 6 to 17. But women also commit hands-on offenses; rough estimates put the rate of paedophilic attraction at 1 to 4% in both men and women. Studies suggest that a small subset of male and female paedophiles have an interest in toddlers, or even infants. I haven't heard of female paedophilic doctors though. I must look it up. I bet there aren't any."

"The bloody internet makes it so much easier. Images of child sex abuse have reached a crisis point on the internet, spreading at unprecedented rates in part because tech platforms and law enforcement agencies have failed to keep pace with the problem."

"Yes. Like the 18 months the British police took to catch Myles Bradbury when the Canadian police would have arrested him straight away."

"The Canadian guys appear to be pretty punchy. Elucidating and working on their cases straight away."

"Probably comes from the great training they get. Remember the reputation of the Canadian mounted police?"

"They got on to Fred Janke smartly."

"Who was he?" "

"A doctor from Sylvan Lake, Alta, Canada who had been practising family medicine for nearly 30 years. He faced charges related to child pornography after an investigation by police in two Canadian provinces.

He was aged 62 when he was finally arrested in Edmonton after investigation by the Alberta Law Enforcement Response Team's Internet child exploitation unit and the police in Victoria.

Police had been investigating a website known to host online chat rooms geared toward child sex, and once they determined the suspect was based in Alberta the information was referred to authorities there.

"How did they finally catch him?"

"He was engaged in sexually explicit online conversations with an adult and had attempted to arrange to have sex with that person's five-year-old daughter. The daughter did not exist and the man was actually speaking with a Victoria police undercover operator."

"Glad they got the pervert. Love it,"

"Janke is facing charges of making arrangements to commit sexual offences against a child, making child pornography and distribution of child pornography.

"What a problem. So many sick people."

"Is it the current world we live in or were they made that way?"

"May be the current world facilitates it. The number of child sex abuse image offences being recorded by police has risen by almost a quarter. The government threatens to regulate web giants if they do not crack down on the phenomenon."

"Yes it's the internet that accommodates chat rooms and sex sites. Before you just had to walk into the sex shops to get what you wanted. Before I met you and your taught angular body I had to rely on visual aids" Fi opened her mouth and shut it again as he said this in pretend surprise

"I've got a collection of pornographic videos. Straight sex; a bit of lesbianism; that sort"

"I forgive you" Fi said "No paedophilia?"

"Oh God no. Although on statistics I should be. Paedophiles are committing crimes at least once every 23 minutes in England and Wales Fi according to Google and I guess those are the ones that are known about."

"I cannot understand anyone who has been around children wanting to view them in this light" "Loads out there Fi. A total of more than 22,700 offences were recorded in 2017/18, up by 23 per cent on the previous year. Offences included taking, distributing and possessing indecent images of children."

"Don't these people have a heart?" Yvan said it in an aggrieved voice

"Some do. I remember reading an article once where this little girl was forced into a sexual relationship with the man who was her mother's sexual partner, her 'pseudo' step dad" He subsequently hanged himself and it came out in the investigation that the little girl had said to him " We need to tell Mummy that you and I are getting married"

I wrote this poem about it called "The stars on the little girls ceiling".

"Recite the poem to me Fi?"

"I'll have to look it up."

"I'm restless. Can you get it now? My mind is wandering to awful paedophiles and the creative ways they entrap children."

 "Ok I'll get my mobile phone. I was driving to one of my infernal jobs. I was on the M1 motorway. Miles of driving to get to jobs; the poem came to me as I had just read the article in the gutter press. It made me sad. I placed my mobile phone on the front seat of the car to record my thoughts and the composition. You can hear the road noise as background to the poem. I composed it while driving along.

"I'm all ears Fi" Fi found her phone and played the recording to Yvan.

<u>The stars on the little girls ceiling</u>

He robbed the stars from the little girls ceiling.

 He robbed the stars with his body heaving

Blocking her vision, blocking her light.

Choking her face in the dead of the night

When he had left her all she could see,

 were the stars on the ceiling through her misery

The stars on the ceiling did not make her stop

 Feeling his weight or the feel of his .ock

The stars were pink they glowed in the dark.

 The stars are now gone. They are part of her past.

They had twinkled once on the little girls ceiling.

 They may have helped in her process of healing

Until this day he has gone unpunished.

 She cannot complain, she can die but not perish

The father who uses his child for perversion

 Can only be cured by extreme castration

Not only of genitals, hormones and slime

 But removal of that deviant mind.

There was a hush in the room as she finished reading. Fi looked up; then silently switched off her phone.

"Yes bring back Capital punishment. It makes me feel empty Fi. The suffering these children have to endure" His eyes were mesmerising Fi yet again.

 "Fi I curse them. Curse these fathers who abuse their children. I saw what you wrote about Lawrence and his father, in your book 'Murder in Medicine'. Awful."

Yvan stayed quiet for a moment. He thought, then questioned

"Was that you? It seems close to home?"

"No I've never been sexually abused by relatives but the mother of one of my daughters friends told me she had been raped by an Indian Uncle. She never got over it. She became an alcoholic. I've suspected others of sexually abusing their children and in one case I know of I think he is being punished by God as he now has pancreatic cancer.. This poem is for all the children out there who were abused by their fathers, male and female alike."

"Did you put this poem in your book 'Naughty poems for naughty people'? I don't remember reading it."

"No this is the first time I'm putting it in print. This form of depravity was too deep for that Poetry book. Those poems were just funny and erotic"

"What leads these paedophiles who are doctors to do these acts? Doctors are supposed to be caring professionals." Yvan's eyes looked glacial green in the bright light pouring through into his study.

Fi distracted by his eyes said "What an attractive man you are. Your eyes are the entry to your soul."

Yvan smiling said "Water finds its own level Fi that's why I am here with you. Attractiveness gravitates to attractiveness"

"How can paedophiles be trusted in the general population? They are perverts. Are they allowed to work again?"

"Nicholas Spicer did. He was another of those non hands-on paedophiles. He escaped being struck off in 2010 even though he was described by the General Medical Council as a 'deviant' for downloading child-sex stories.

He read the paedophile fantasies on his home computer between 2003 and 2007 while working with children as a GP but was cleared of misconduct and allowed to go back to work in another part of the country following a six-month ban.

"The GMC again; making insane decisions. Is he not exposed to children in his next practice?"

"You know my feelings on the doctors ruling body, the GMC which is filled with lawyers who just want a case win not common sense about doctors"

"I know your feelings on the GMC's standard attitude to cases. 'The law is an arse' is a frequently quoted parlance."

 "He probably appeared obsequious, apologetic and grovelling to the tribunal. So he is allowed to go somewhere else and practice"

"Some perverts are released to practice. They can't be supervised that closely."

 "Benjamin Obukofe certainly was. He was found guilty by a court last year of sexually assaulting two colleagues at Spire Hospital in Leicestershire, including a girl of 17." Yvan looked at her in surprise

"Although the married father was given a suspended prison sentence and put on the sex offenders register for seven years, he has not been struck off and will be free to work within a year."

"I guess 17 is nearly at the legal age limit. That's why he got a light sentence Fi?"

"His is a straightforward case of inappropriate sexual behaviour. These doctors don't seem to know their boundaries" Yvan was shaking his head and tut-tutting.

"The fact that they are doctors is 'by the by'. They are in the Epstein, Harvey Weinstein film director category. Just sick, sexually-predatory men who think they can get away with anything and happen to have chosen medicine as their profession."

"In the film industry I can understand it. Actresses and the casting couch of the director but in medicine?"

"The Yorkshire Ripper" was a bible reader Yvan. Perverts abound everywhere."

"And when he wasn't going to church and reading the bible the Yorkshire Ripper was killing prostitutes in North England Fi"

"Christ's follower Mary Magdalen was a prostitute. Christ never said a word against her."

"There is difficulty for people with strong religious beliefs and the attraction of the flesh Fi. The eternal dilemma, consigned to the box of life experiences." His gaze narrowed

"You are like that. You obviously enjoy sex but try your best to keep it under control because of your religion"

"Tantric sex is more exciting Yvan. No need for condoms. Pseudo unprotected sex and visual turn-ons are so much better." Fi was purring with pleasure at the thought.

"Do you really want to get married before we have full penetrative sex?"

"Yes. It's what I did with the Scientologist" Yvan arched a brow

"Non-penetrative sex is much more pleasurable." Fi said subtly

"Sometimes I can't believe I have you in my life. I am so lucky. I would suffer cataclysmic trauma if you left. I am waiting for when I will make love to my wife."

"Then you will just have to put up with the boredom of what we do together till you get executive level burnout."

"It's not a high pressure job Fi servicing you and I'm very good with my tongue and hands."

Fi looked at Yvan with pretend innocence. "You do know what to do Yvan. I'm always fascinated as to how you became so expert?"

"It's easy enough. Especially when you are lifting your hips squirming and saying 'Don't stop'

He reached out to her, his right hands tearing at her blouse and pulling her bra off her breasts which tumbled out and rose to his touch. His head bent as he pulled her forward nuzzling licking and pinching tightly. Fi moaned her breathing coming faster as he unzipped her skirt and tore at her underwear.

She lay back, legs akimbo over the arms of the chair as he knelt down and gave homage with his tongue.

Within moments she was squirming, pushing his head in toward her centre till he nearly suffocated. Buried in her he heard her crying out 'Don't stop. Don't stop' then a long moan

Later they lay arms entwined still talking about all the strangely bizarre cases of sexually active doctors.

"It's like you and me together here and now. Something turns them on and then they follow their minds or should I say mindless visions and possibilities of what could be but direct their sexual focus towards their patients."

"Mmm. No embarrassment at their frustrations and behaviour. They seem unable to curb their rogue desires. Most of them are married. Don't their wives give them sex?

" Not the type they want. I just do not understand these men. They should curse themselves when they realise where their minds are going. Instead they go with it, fuel it, fan their flames and live the moment."

Yvan brushed his lips across the nape of her neck. "Like this?"

"Maybe much more than that? Much much more? Maybe less? Some people are more harmless than that. Just sexually inappropriate. Let me tell you about one of them. He was a bible reader as well. Crazy goon."

"Oh no, the difficult chasm between religion and sex rears its head again Fi." Yvan groaned "The Yorkshire Ripper is yet another one of those examples of religion conflicting with sexual desire Fi. All the religious doctors seem to be hypocrites too like the Yorkshire Ripper who read the Bible and killed prostitutes."

"Maybe the Bible reading made him believe he could kill prostitutes?"

"Made him think he was virtuous Fi."

6.   THE VIRTUOUS SEX ADDICT

"That's what I think. Religious doctors appear to have split personalities or at least split lives. The religion doesn't help them control their sexuality. A married Christian doctor Dr Stuart Creed, aged 51, is fighting for his career after facing charges of sexual misconduct. He allegedly hugged a female patient after telling her she was 'very hot'.

Two women reported the Cambridge dermatologist to the General Medical Council.

"You see Yvan. I told you all the doctors in Cambridge were weird. And some people from there too. I met a guy from Cambridge who wanted a sex change operation and spent his life on cruise ships. That was weird"

 Dr. Stuart Creed was 'overfamiliar' He taught the Bible to children in two local church groups. He made various unsolicited advances towards two Patients called A and B by the Medical Practitioners Tribunal Service (MPTS) who judged eight allegations of sexual misconduct against Dr Creed.

Patient A, who had been signed off work with anxiety and had suffered hair loss, was allegedly described by the GP as 'really fit'. She accused Dr Creed of asking 'how many times a week' she had sex during one home visit, and said that she would find another partner 'very easily'. Dr Creed also allegedly confessed to 'really caring' for Patient A 'as a person' and said she was 'perfect' in March 2017. She accused Dr Creed of telling her during one consultation: 'Maybe I shouldn't say that but I really like you as a person. And also saying 'I know this is wrong but you're very hot - can I give you a hug?'   He also attended her home more than once despite her saying that she was happy to go to Dr Creed's practice.

"What was wrong with him? Why did he have to hit on patients? What was his problem?"

 "On or around March 30, 2017, he attended Patient A's home and said: 'You should stop worrying, you are perfect the way you are'; 'I have tried in [sic] other occasions to let you know that I feel something. It is difficult for me to say';'I really care about you, you know that. Maybe I shouldn't say that but I really like you as a person';"

"He sounds like a lonely frustrated single man"

"He wasn't. He was married"

"Meanwhile, psoriasis-stricken Patient B accused the doctor of giving compliments about her appearance and saying she looked 'lovely and just fine'.   Dr Creed unexpectedly turned up at the car showroom at which she worked for unscheduled 'consultations'.   Both women accuse Dr Creed of asking inappropriate and probing questions about their sexual lives."

"Was he targetting them both serially or at the same time?"

"Sequentially. Between October 2017 and February 2018, with Patient B at Buckden Surgery, he told her: 'I don't know what you're worrying about, you look just fine'; She was 'lovely' and 'just right'; 'I think your hair looks nice'; 'It doesn't matter as you aren't having sex anyway'.

"Was the patient married?"

"Separated. On October 3, 2017, during a consultation with Patient B at the Surgery after she split from her husband, Dr Creed said: 'Oh well I think he's an idiot because you look lovely'.

"All of that sounds fairly innocent Fi"

"Yes but it's his further behaviour that is bizarre. In March 2018 Dr Creed attended Patient B's workplace more than once, sat down by her, asked about her job, and told her that he had been by to see her a few times but she was busy. He also drove slowly past her window.

"Yes he is inappropriate to say the least. What is his wife doing all this time?"

"Probably not giving him sex? Around April 2018, without any clinical justification, he called Patient B more than once, left her a voicemail, and even texted her phone."

"So his actions attempted to engage in an inappropriate emotional relationship with Patients A and B?"

"This one was hard for me to judge Yvan. He was obviously odd, sexually motivated, and desirous of something but was it harmless?"

"Are doctors allowed to be sexually inappropriate?"

"Absolutely not. Not even in their speech"

"So he was out of place and shouldn't be able to practice anymore till he sorts out his psychosexual side and stops being inappropriate."

7.   TALKING DIRTY

"My obstetrician used to make inappropriate remarks to me. When I went to consultations he would make remarks not relevant to my pregnancy."

"Like what?"

"Sexual innuendo. I can't even remember now. Comments and jokes that could be construed as sexual in nature. Jokes about how I came to be pregnant."

"His name was Kypros Nicolaides. I thought he made hilariously funny comments. I was a young attractive mother with no obvious husband in sight. He was a colleague as I was working at Kings at the time. He contrasted starkly with Donald Gibb another obstetrician in the department who was a sweet serious guy who delivered my third child."

"Kypros doesn't seem harmful. Verbal slap and tickle."

" That was what I thought but one patient however took dislike to his behaviour and he ended up facing the General Medical Council. He should never have been reported unlike some doctors who are quite gross in their verbal content."

"I'll look it up for you because I can't remember the details off the top of my head. Kypros made the press. I have had many doctors making sexually inappropriate comments to me. I think they just want to be sexually arousing to attractive women. Kypros was just funny."

"Time passes with you Fi. I never wonder how I am going to get through the next few hours or look for an escape."

Kypros had been accused of making flippant and offensive remarks to a woman patient whose unborn twins died in an operation he carried out. But Professor Kyprianos Nicolaides told the GMC that he was in tears after the babies' death which he called a "human tragedy" for both their mother Jennifer Sabin and for himself.

"I don't think she would have complained if the babies hadn't died Yvan. He was an expert on foetal medicine. For once the GMC got it right. They cleared him of serious professional misconduct."

"Didn't you tell me you dressed sexily Fi? Was that why the guys were hitting on you?"

"Maybe but patients don't need to be harassed because they are sexually provocatively dressed. Dr David Jones operated a family medicine practice and is supposed to have made sexually inappropriate remarks from 2009 but wasn't reported till 2016"

During a medical appointment with a patient in August 2009, Jones commented on the patient's appearance during an intimate exam. And during another he inquired about the patient's interest in obtaining a tattoo in her vaginal area.

"In my mind that puts questions on the patient" Yvan said strongly. "Which normal person wants to have that area tattooed?" He shuddered

"Rather weak reason to haul him up though don't you think?"

"It was Jones's first time before the discipline committee, but he had been cautioned by the College several times before.

In 2009, the complaints committee cautioned him for a "breach in boundaries" in a physician-patient relationship involving self-disclosure of a personal nature to a patient.

"That seems harmless enough?"

At that time he reported to the College that he attended its boundaries course in 2008.

"That's weird. He goes for a course to learn about boundaries in the doctor patient relationship and it hasn't taught him anything. He continues his behaviour?"

 "Yes he is someone who doesn't learn. Again in 2010, he was cautioned for asking a patient, who was there for an unrelated matter, questions of a sexual nature and for the use of a profane word."

"Which one?"

"They didn't say but I think it was F>U>C>K."

"Really? That word isn't profane" Yvan said. "It originated from Fornication Under Consent of King. The British introduced it into the Oxford dictionary"

"Don't think you can explain that to patients Yvan"

"What are your professional boundaries then?"

"It is obvious that doctors are going to have natural human attractions just like anyone else, including sexual or romantic feelings towards their colleagues, patients or others they come into contact with. However, the prohibition on doctors entering into emotional or sexual relationships with patients (and relatives of patients) is one that most people endorse and which has good public policy reasons for it to be strictly policed. Colleagues too ought to be able to go to work without being harassed and exposed to sexualised behaviour. And in the community in which a doctor lives, people have a right not to be sexually harassed."

"I love your telling me so much about your personal experiences Fi. Have you experienced this?"

"Never an attraction to a patient but I reported one of my colleagues once to the medical director of the trust. The medical director said "We have addressed your concerns" and that was all.

"Why didn't it go any further? What did he do?"

"He used to look at images of naked women on his computer in the afternoons when he should have been working. They examined his computer and found evidence of it and just told him to 'refrain in the future'."

"He also made inappropriate comments to me about his daughter having a tongue piercing; said she would give great oral sex."

"Did you tell the medical director all of this?"

"Yes. I found out later they were friends. That's why nothing happened. Easy to turn a blind eye if the offending doctor is your chum."

"Did he ever grab you?"

"I can't remember if he groped me but a Zimbabwe guy I worked with certainly did.   He was a handsome guy; intelligent. Got an MBA in business studies while working with me but, as you put it 'brains in his bollocks' Every time we were alone together he tried to pull me towards him, kiss me, or fondle me and usually he did this in the clinical consulting rooms. He had a wife and 4 children at home but wanted to have sex with me in the on-call rooms. Those on-call rooms did see a lot of sex."

"Did you sample him? They are supposed to be well slung"

 "I was married at the time and would not have a casual encounter with a married man even if I weren't. What do you think of me, even asking me that question?"

Slowly and tenderly Yvan caressed her lip with his finger seeing that Fi had got angry. Still experiencing her displeasure he said

"Did I tell you about the black guy with the big wang?"

Fi, successfully distracted said "No"

"The black guy is chatting up a sex goddess as a potential conquest. He buys her the most expensive champagne on the bar list. She is not interested. He tells her about his job, CEO of a large city start-up company, she is not interested. He asks her to see where he lives in Canary wharf in a multimillion penthouse apartment. She is still not interested His income and wealth do not interest her. She tries to discourage him. Finally he says "I've got the biggest member you will ever see"

Fi's attention is arrested by the story line. Yvan continues "The black sex goddess's attention is held. She asks, sitting up alertly "How long is it?"

 He replies "Six inches"

Black sex goddess sits back disappointed "That's not very long. I've had men with longer"

The reply comes "Six inches from the ground baby" A surprised laugh burst from Fi at the answer.

"Go on Fi tell me about these sex crazed doctors"

Not sure how well-endowed Dr Zimbabwe was but another stupid doctor at a different hospital hired a prostitute on a night that he was meant to be doing on-call.

"Ah the tales and screams from those on-call rooms would make a separate story Fi or a poem. Try and make up one now."

"Ok. Let me think"

"Let's call it 'The Tale of the on-call Room'

Fi thought. "You'll have to give me some time till I get the rhythm and cadence of it Yvan. Do you have any particular preference? Haiku? Limerick? Quadruplet? Couplet?"

"A tale I think like the 'Highwayman' poem"

"What's the trade-off for all this mental activity?

"What about physical activity later to satisfy your great hungry appetite?"

"Ok. Poem, food, bed, sex."

"Deal"

Fi started thinking and writing in her notepad. Yvan studied the stockmarket.

She looked up at him laughing "Got it"

Yvan's countenance expressed surprise. "So quickly?"

"Uhuh"

"Well?"

Who is in here tonight? To cover my walls with crime

The gynaecologist with his speculum or the young lad in his prime

 Whatever it is whatever they do I always enjoy the view

For I am the wall of the on-call room and see them whenever they scr.w

Yvan laughed "Disgusting use of commonality Fi"

"Grand remonstrance?" He said nothing

8.   HOOKER SEX

 "Tell me about the guy who used the on-call room for sex Fi"

The air-conditioned hospital on call room was as still as the grave and as uninviting. Somewhere beyond the window, the sun climbed above the hottest day in the UK. Lying there in his scrubs having just made contact with his escort Rupert couldn't stop anxiety as he clenched his teeth. Fear and anticipation went through him.

Dr Rupert Pemsel, from Compton in Winchester was 33 at the time' a trainee anaesthetist and his wife Sheyi a GP aged 40 was pregnant. He was branded "abhorrent" after he paid for sex with a 29 year old hooker Leanne Kennedy, in an on-call room while still wearing his scrubs.

Pemsel claimed the 40-minute encounter at Princess Anne Hospital in Southampton in December 2013 was to curb "stress" he suffered at work and after helping sick kids in Uganda.

"Stock excuses. Did someone find him in his on call room? Did he do it because his wife was pregnant and didn't give him sex?"

"He had 2 previous children so I'm not sure about that. Pregnancy made me even more sexually rapacious so I'm not sure he could use the excuse that his wife wasn't giving him sex.

"Then why did he do it?"

"On-call rooms in hospital are soul-destroying. It's like being a patient on the ward. I hated them. Lonely places. No TV; just a bed, chair and a sink; similar to Nelson Mandela's cell on Roben Island.

"But I never thought of having sex in them. It takes a certain mind-set." Fi said pointedly

 "Did the shouts of mirth and moans, alert somebody?"

"Inbetween him helping with emergency caesareans? No"

Dr Pemsel says he was addicted to pornography and told a tribunal he wanted to take his obsession to the next level with the 40-minute session with the call girl at Southampton's Princess Anne Hospital.

He would never have been found out but was exposed after the prostitute tried to blackmail him out of £10,000 and he went to the police.

The trainee anaesthetist texted the woman before their encounter admitting their liaison would be "naughty" and "discretion would be appreciated".

"So she spotted opportunity to make a lot more money without having to put-out?"

 "I don't think he had that much money to pay. Certainly didn't want to give it to a blackmailer. After the blackmail attempt, Pemsel came clean to his wife Sheyi, and reported the threats to the police.

 Subsequently the blackmailer made contact with Pemsel. He alerted the police who assigned two inspectors to mount a sting operation to trap the culprits at the Hilton Hotel, Basingstoke, on January 6 2014.

 Leanne Kennedy, also known as Leanne Davies, and a younger man were arrested and pleaded guilty to blackmail.

"Was that just one offence?"

"As far as I can tell it was. When they examined Rupert Pemsell's phone, as the police usually do all they found was photographs of a patient's radiograph on his iPhone which depicted a bottle up the man's bottom."

"I guess he could show that to friends as after dinner conversation" Yvan said

"Yes. Those photo's were for his own amusement."

"What happened to him?"

"His activity was pretty harmless. His pregnant wife probably came to the hearings to win sympathy so he got off lightly. He kept his job and of course he was apologetic. That is the key when you go before these panels. Be apologetic"

"You know that but you never apologised to the GMC."

"Yes true. I lost £3,000 a week because my pride wouldn't let me apologise. I'd rather tell the GMC to f-ck off"

"Well I know money doesn't matter to you. You live like a pauper. What did Pemsel say?"

Pemsel confessed: "Patients would have been appalled and shocked to find out that their doctor, whilst on-call and supposedly ready to respond to life-threatening emergencies, was engaged in their own sexual gratification with an escort in the hospital they were being treated at.

"This is a total abuse of my position and I am, and always will be, utterly ashamed of it.

"By doing so I failed to put my patients first, I abused their trust and I damaged their confidence in the profession."

He escaped with just a ten-month suspension rather than being struck off the medical register.

When he reappeared before the disciplinary panel at a later date they agreed he could return to work when his 10 month suspension expires. He is now planning a new career as a family GP.

"Easy for him to get hookers into a GP surgery isn't it?"

"I think he has learnt his lesson Yvan"

He told the Medical Practitioners Tribunal Service he had now learnt to cope with stress by cycling and using mindfulness exercises, which he described as 'life changing.

He was also studying for a diploma in stress management and using his experiences to help colleagues manage their own work pressures.

'"Did his romp with the escort while working on a maternity ward teach him a lesson?"

"He appears to have swapped prostitutes and porn - for cycling. Some people choose cycling from the start although my daughter once said to me all men on bikes are gay"

Outside the house the sun blazed relentlessly, a rare occurrence in Britain.

"Come on dorogoy time for a walk. Only time will tell whether Pemsel is abstaining from pornography, and whether his vow never to use an escort again is kept."

While walking on Albert Bridge heading for Battersea Park, Yvan who had not said anything till then suddenly blurted out

"Doctors are ordinary men Fi. All men want to go to prostitutes and have things done to them that their wives would never do."

"Did you? Go to a prostitute?"

"My first sexual encounter was in Soho. I was too respectful of all the girls at school and had never had sex or even kissed someone"

"What happened?" Yvan looked little-boyish as he spoke

"The prostitute stole my money and my credit card and I had no way of getting home so I had to call my mother"

Fi doubled up laughing at Yvan's facial expression

"It was a mental 'Mama's ruler treatment.' I never did it again"

"I'm not saying doctors shouldn't go to prostitutes or look at porn off duty if they can't get sex any other way Yvan but when they are in hospital it should be a sacred place almost like a church; sacrosanct. You should only focus on the job."

"Perhaps pray for strength not to offend?"

"Don't tease me Yvan. They should pray if they are thinking of doing something that will cost them their job. I think they do misuse hospital premises and quite often don't get found out."

Yvan pulled Fi's hand towards him and gently caressing it said "Don't walk so fast. Remember I have a stroke."

Fi stopped walking and they both leant on the bridge. Fi stared into the water of the River Thames. Yvan's hair was tousled by the breeze over the river

"Reminds me of Dr Robert Barnett, who worked at Milton Keynes University Hospital. He admitted spending the night with a prostitute in Poland but it only came to light because he was convicted of stealing a handbag. I'm not sure whether the GMC struck him off for the criminal conviction, hooker sex or both.

"I remember being offered £500 for an overnight session with someone who mistakenly thought I was 'on the make' when I was parked outside 55 Beauchamp Place. He was a nice looking guy and I may even have done it for free with him. I was in the throes of divorce and any sexual encounter would have been quite heartening but caution prevailed. "

"Tell me more. You weren't dreaming?"

Fi thought back to the encounter.

Fi was just driving away with Cas when she saw Shen, her Afro carribbean neighbour sitting in his Range Rover with two white women. Both looked in their twenties and she had never seen them before.

She wound down the window of the car curiosity getting the better of her.

"Shen, hey how goes. Where is Lania?"

"She's gone to Venice on holiday"

"Who are these girls?"

"You are forward" Yvan said when she told him. "Haven't you heard about MYOB?"

"What's that?"

"Mind Your Own Business"

"No not for me. I'd make a good investigative journalist"

"What did he say to your question?"

"Oh just some friends"

Cas hysterically shouted "Mum we are late. Give Shen the Spanish inquisition later"

As Fi wound up the window of her car she heard Shen say ' 55 Beauchamp Place' punching the address into his sat nav.

After Fi had dropped Cas she searched for 55 Beauchamp Place on her sat nav and drove to it. She found herself passing Harrods.

She pulled over and looked at the building. There was a restaurant on the ground floor.

Disappointed she thought 'Shen's just taking friends out to dinner. Ah well nothing to report to Lania. Harmless activity.'

Then she looked up to the first floor of the 3 storey Victorian building. The first floor room had a number of young scantily clad white-skinned European women wearing negligee's through which underwear was clearly visible. She watched them. Some were smoking cigarettes through cigarette holders. They were strangely attired for the middle of winter.

A greying man in his forties or perhaps early fifties came out from the ground floor door and crossed the road. Quick as a flash Fi jumped out of the car and accosted him. She smiled.

"Hi. Can I ask you something?"

"Sure but it's cold. Can we sit in my car?" Fi could see him eyeing her. His gaze was mentally undressing her and weighing her up. High heeled boots, black tights, short skirt, breasts protruding through the open fur lined coat. Pretty face.

"Let's sit in mine" she said. They got in and she switched the car engine on and turned up the heating

"What is that place that you came out of?" He leaned across Fi and pointed to the first floor

"It's a place you go for sex"

"Prostitutes?"

"It's advertised as an escort agency in Yellow pages. The girls decide whether they want to have sex with you. You take them out to dinner and then depending on the negotiations and the price they want you can have them for a few hours or the whole night" He kept staring at Fi. His eyes were disconcerting. Penetrating blue but with thick dark lashes. He spoke with an American accent but had lightly tanned Mediterranean skin.

"Why are you alone then?"

"They are all pink and horribly thin. No one has fed them pasta. I didn't like the choice"

"Are you Italian?"

"Ancestry. I live in Tennessee. I'm here on business, staying 2 nights at the Ritz."

He reached in his pocket, his gaze exceptionally friendly, and brought out a roll of 100 dollar bills and his business card. Brandishing it he said "I like you though. Would a thousand dollars entice you into staying the night with me?"

"Thousand dollars" Yvan said faintly

"In my emotional state Yvan, not realising that I could lock the thousand dollars in my car and hand the key to the concierge of the Ritz I made the wrong decision. I needed that money and the sex. I had paid half a million in divorce fees to lawyers to try and save my two London houses in the divorce."

Yvan looked up at the solitary aeroplane circling without looking at Fi.

"He was attractive Yvan. He smelt of expensive cigarette smoke and looked like a great Levithian and those eyes were really something. I would have loved to have had them looking down on me while he was inside me. I was too timorous." Fi remembered it. Without taking notice of Yvan who was still staring up at the sky, she continued.

I said "I'm sorry I don't do that sort of thing."

"Can anything persuade you to change your mind? Two nights? Same rate?"

Fi looked at him, laughed whimsically and said "God will punish me"

He said "God brought us together. Sex doesn't count in his eyes."

"I'm sorry." Fi said. He interrupted her "Julian. My name is Julian"

"I can't come with you." Fi kissed him on the cheek feeling sorry for him and for herself. "I must go now. Lovely to meet you"

Getting out of the car he said "I'm in room 29 if you change your mind"

Fi and Yvan had a pleasant walk around Battersea Park. When they were walking back to his house Yvan said "Why did Robert Barnett steal the Polish prostitutes handbag?

 "In Dr Barnett's case I thought he just wanted his money back after buying the sex from her. That's why he stole her handbag. Wonder whether he paid £500 to her?"

"I'd give you £500 Fi. I'd match his rate, a thousand dollars"

"It'll cost you much more than that Yvan. I need the wedding ring on my finger but in the long term your investment will pay off as after that you get it for free."

"Ok. Let's go to Gretna Green tomorrow. I'll buy you a Cartier diamond ring as we pass by Harrods on our way"

"Let me check on what happened in Robert Barnett's case when we get home not sure whether I've got the details quite right.

Fi did an internet search and said. "Oops. I'm wrong. He didn't steal her bag. It was someone else's. He was just a bad un; trying to recoup his losses from sex by robbing another person in the hotel.

"It's a warning to the public. They should not trust a doctor"

After dinner Yvan tells Maria the housekeeper to leave and asks Fi to come and lie in bed beside him. His behaviour puzzled Fi.

"What's wrong?"

"The green-eyed-monster has got me."

"Jealousy is a very damaging and destructive force which can irreparably damage love. Who are you jealous of?"

"Julian. He attracted you. He was young and handsome. Do you still have his business card?"

"Yvan. You can't be; that was 7 years ago. I never contacted him and I'll have to upturn my house looking for the business card now. I'm not sure about jealous business men but jealous doctors are very dangerous"

"Who are you thinking of?"

"Someone who worked where my niece who is a doctor in Texas practised. The cancer hospital is world famous. It's in the University of Texas, the M.D. Anderson Hospital. The 43 year old doctor, Ana Maria Gonzalez-Angulo, worked there with Dr. George Blumenschein at this world-renowned breast Cancer Center.

"What crime did she commit?" Yvan said, completely distracted from his own jealousy.

"She spiked her lover's coffee with a chemical found in antifreeze ethylene glycol on Jan. 27, 2013, after he spurned her in favour of his long-time girlfriend. The trial was in Houston, Texas. Ana Gonzalez-Angulo, was on a criminal charge of aggravated assault by poisoning

9.   CONFERENCE SEX

"I guess it is easy to fall in love with people you work with" Yvan said.

"Women need a steady partner to keep them from being attracted to their colleagues."

"And men?"

"Depends on their loyalty. Blumenschein, who was 50 years old, was living with his longtime girlfriend, Evette Toney, when the love triangle started with Ana Gonzalez-Angulo sitting in Blumenschein's lap as they worked on scholarly papers. He called her his "Little Princess." He began the sexual relationship with Gonzalez-Angulo in September 2011 after working closely with her for several months."

 "How do you move from flirting, into a sexual relationship?

 "For them it happened in a hotel room on a business trip to Stockholm, Sweden. Although if a woman sits on your lap at the outset you know what will happen sooner or later."

"Have you ever done that?"

"Sat on my colleagues lap. No never?"

"No. Had sex at a conference?"

Fi looked embarrassed "Yes I did but it was because my ex-husband was there, cavorting around. We were in the same field of Medicine so attended conferences together unless we decided to split the workload and he'd go one year and I the other. On that one occasion when I had conference sex we had gone to the same one together as now we were divorcing.   I wanted to show that I could do conference sex as well.

"I like that term 'conference sex.'

"I'll tell you that story after I finish this one"

All jealousy had disappeared from Yvan. The temporary division between them had been displaced by her physical contact and closeness. The child in the man was reconnected with his life source.

Medical conferences took the Gonzalez-Angulo/ Blumenschein pairing to Dubai, Vietnam and even Colombia, where Blumenschein met the parents of his mistress.

"She will want more Fi won't she? She doesn't want to be a mistress when she is old and aging"

"Like me Yvan. Without that ring I am.."

"Aging fanny?" he interrupted

Fi laughed saying" You are shocking. My name is Fi not Fanny"

She could see Yvan was happy again

Blumenschein had more than a year of clandestine casual sexual encounters but Ana wanted more. She developed a "fatal attraction" and wanted to bear Blumenschein's children.

"At 43 years of age? Could she?"

"Not sure about Colombian women but if you have regular periods you could still be ovulating and fertile till you are aged 50. It is quite common for Asian women to be able to procreate until age 55."

Ana saw her goal slipping away because he was using in vitro fertilization to try to conceive a child with, Toney his partner who testified at trial that   she had a miscarriage while pregnant with twins in the same year the affair started.

"No wonder they had to have in- vitro fertilisation" Yvan remarked. "He is losing sperm to his mistress."

"It's replaced soon enough Yvan but maybe now he can't get it up with Evette Toney?"

When Ana realized Blumenschein was trying to start a family with Evette she decided to make her move.

She invited him over for a cup of "special Colombian coffee" on the morning of Jan. 27, 2013. It was much too sweet for the doctor, who preferred his coffee black.

Blumenschein said he started feeling "tipsy" after drinking the "sickeningly sweet" coffee.

"I could easily poison you Fi because you love sweet drinks"

"I'm hoping that won't be necessary Yvan. I've shot my bolt with you. I'm not having any more men after you; too exhausting."

"You haven't had me yet"

"You have captured my soul. That should do for now; and soon you will have the aging body. This is only the warm-up."

A day after Blumenschein was hospitalized, a kidney doctor at M.D. Anderson tested his urine and used a cell-phone to take a picture of the microscopic crystals he found.

Doctors and experts later testified the photo showed ethylene glycol, the toxic chemical in anti-freeze and commonly found in medical labs.

That photo of crystals, along with Blumenschein's testimony, sealed Gonzalez-Angulo's fate.

Witness after witness for the prosecution described what they saw Blumenschein eat and drink in the days leading up to the poisoning. They even called the owner of Niko Niko's, the Montrose restaurant where he ordered a take-away the day before. They all said it was not possible for that food to have any substance that could have caused the crystals

After hearing from 22 witnesses, jurors decided Gonzalez-Angulo put the toxic chemical in the mug, rebuffing her lawyers claim that the sweetener was nothing but Splenda and that someone else poisoned him.

"What did his partner Toney think about it all?"

He admitted his infidelity to Evette while in his hospital bed. They began recording calls with Ana to trap her. They feared her.

"On multiple occasions, she told me she'd kill anyone who got in her way," Blumenschein testified. He and other witnesses said she spoke of having paid people in Colombia to kill those who had harmed her relatives. Blumenschein said he believed her. He feared for his life

"What was her sentencing?"

"Blumenschein's stated that the black coffee damaged his kidneys. The oncologist testified that he has only 40% of his kidney function and had to undergo emergency dialysis to survive and that the poisoning would likely shorten his life; or mean that he could require the need for a kidney transplant in the future."

"So?"

"They asked for a 30 year prison sentence"

"Did she get that?"

"A steady stream of patients, colleagues and family members testified in her defence to prevent it."

One patient said "She saved my life, and I always felt like she would save a whole lot of lives"

"She tried to kill someone" Yvan said" She should go to jail"

"That's what the jurors thought. Prosecutors reminded jurors throughout the trial that the victim is also a cancer doctor who saves lives."

They said "Don't feel bad for one second about sending her to prison. She did that herself."

"This story is better than a TV soap opera." Yvan said delightedly

"It was much watched in Texas and made international headlines, especially in Ana's homeland Colombia, where reporters clamoured for details after the verdict was handed down."

"What did she get?"

"Ten years and costs"

"Did Toney stay with Blumenschein?

"He had lived with Evette Toney since 2007. Now he needed her because of his ill health, she decided to stay. Yes they are still together. Women are very forgiving."

"Ana gets out of prison in 2024." Yvan said. "Do you think she will call it quits?"

"Anyone with common sense would but I suspect she is deranged and may try to get revenge"

"And now I want your conference sex story Fi"

"We were at...

"No. I want a story"

Fi is in Singapore for the International Society of Haematology Conference. Hot air surrounds her. She basks in it. Her skimpy clothes show off her breasts and legs. There are plenty of good looking men arrived from all over the world. Soo Lai walks up to her on the first day of the conference. She appears to be on a mission. "Hey Fi, I saw Maz at the Thalassaemia conference. He didn't stay for the full three days. He left early. Took a flight somewhere else. Did he tell you?"

"What do you mean Soo Lai? Are you saying he went with another woman?"

"There were three of them leaving the conference early. Maz was one of them. Davina went on the same plane."

Fi knows Davina, a tall, pretty, leggy, blonde, junior trainee haematologist." Soo Lay says "Oh he didn't tell you?" Having sowed the seeds she walks away nonchalantly.

 For the rest of the day Fi tries to accost Soo Lay and continue the conversation about Maz and what he had done. She had always suspected his infidelities and here was someone giving her evidence of them"

She is distraught. Soo Lai says no more to her. Yes Fi and Maz were planning to divorce but her feelings were mixed about the divorce. She was not sure whether she was doing the correct thing." Could she live with infidelity? Were the children going to suffer? Hard questions to answer. Is any decision the correct one?

Soo Lai was pointing out that others had noticed Maz leaving the conference 2 days earlier and going off with Davina and some other men. Had he been unfaithful? Was he always unfaithful? Her mind was in a whirl.

The first day of the conference ended with Fi not learning a thing about haematological advances. Her mind perseverated on Maz. The Big Pharma company had organised a visit to see the 'Teracotta warriors'. Fi decides to stand in line waiting to view them. A tall slightly overweight young man in glasses is behind her. He starts chatting to her. He introduces himself.

"I am Sven Dahl"

Fi knows the name. He is famous having made a world discovery of blood clotting problems. He can see that she is impressed by who he is and that he is talking to her a humble junior consultant. He has curly auburn hair and looks about late thirties. Fi realises that he is chatting her up. She is flattered. They go into the darkened hall in which the warriors are lined up. He makes every attempt to touch her as they move by the giant stone figures. They go into the next room and sit down for the presentation about the warriors. He puts his arm round the back of her chair leaning in to her intently. He takes her hand in his. He moves her hand into her lap and gradually shifts from sensuously massaging her hand to massaging the insides of her thigh. It has the desired effect. She forgets Maz.

She thinks 'I can do it too' Over the years I went to several conferences and I was always faithful to Maz but now I have an opportunity to experience what it is like. One night at a conference with a world –expert desiring her. Maz wasn't a world expert. She had never done anything like this before. Maybe she should? Sex with a world-discoverer. Is that why all these film directors get actresses in their beds? What is the excitement of sleeping with someone famous?

Sven whispers to her nibbling her ear while he does so "Let's not have the conference dinner Fi. Can I take you out tonight?"

Fi whispers back boldly saying "We could have room service in your room Sven"

She hears his sharp intake of breath.

Fi continues softly "Which hotel are you staying in?" By now his fingers are near the tops of her thighs and probing deeper. She can feel the warm wetness seeping through her dress. He pulls her hand into his lap and lets her feel his hardness. The lights come on in the auditorium and she hastily pulls her hand back.

"I'm at the Mandarin Oriental. What time do you think you will be there?" Sven says

They arrange to meet at 7.30. Fi is so wet she is hardly able to walk normally. Sven too manages to stagger out of the auditorium adjusting himself as he goes.

"Is that enough Yvan" Fi asks

"Oh noo. Don't stop there. What happened?"

"I didn't go Yvan. When I returned to my room to prepare for an evening of sex common sense got the better of me. I couldn't do it even though I was divorcing. I went to the conference dinner instead but couldn't leave him high and dry."

"He was not too pleased I guess. Did he say anything the next day?"

"Well I wanted him to be fed and I didn't want him to wonder where I was so I called his hotel room and told him I was going to the conference dinner instead. He said he would come to it and asked that we be seated together.

"During the meal he tried his best on several occasions to turn me on. Nibbling my ear, stroking my back, putting his hand on my thigh and massaging it. Getting under the serviette on my lap and trying to lift my dress."

"I am surprised others didn't notice"

"They may have done. He was quite open in his technique."

"Technique?"

"It was a technique. I think he was used to going to conferences and having female doctors fall at his feet when he mentioned who he was and what he discovered."

"Did his technique work?"

"It was not his technique but what I'd heard about Maz from Soo Lai that worked. The devil got the better of me and at the end of the evening I agreed to go back to Sven's room."

"Wow. You succumbed?"

"Almost. God intervened. The taxi route back to his hotel took me by my hotel and I decided on the spur of the moment that this was a message that I shouldn't continue to do wrong. I asked the taxi to stop outside my hotel, asked Sven to forgive me but that I had to leave. I gave him a long and deep tongue-encircling kiss and rushed back into my hotel afraid he would follow me"

"Did he?"

"No and he didn't speak to me for the rest of the conference. I was the one that got away."

"Didn't you tell me you were a world discoverer?"

"Yes in malignant diseases not in his field. I was a world expert in my own right but that wasn't why Sven wanted to get in my knickers. He, like most men just wanted to get between these legs. After the word spread that I was getting divorced the whole haematology community and other strange bods like my male cousins started to hit on me"

Yvan was looking chagrined. "You are a prude. Why didn't you just enjoy?"

"Good Catholic upbringing. I wish I did have sex with Sven. I missed my opportunity for conference sex. It would have been revenge"

"You had no extraordinary sexual activities to show for all the years of being married?"

"No. I was faithful and boring."

"From what you told me Maz was doing it every day on his way home from work if opportunity availed itself" Yvan said

"I don't want to think about it Yvan. "

"Were you really faithful for 20 years of marriage?"

"Yes. It wasn't because people weren't continually after me. I was always being chased. "God kept you on the straight and narrow?"

"Not really. I think if one gets married you should not be unfaithful. It was what Paul Newman said about Joanne Woodward. "It doesn't matter where you wet your appetite so long as you eat at home"

"Didn't he also say 'Why eat hamburger outside when you have got steak at home'?"

"He may have done. I didn't hear that one but the principle is the same. Don't get married if you want to be dipping your wick elsewhere."

"The two of you sound dramatically dissimilar in modus operandi you and Maz" Yvan's glance was fixed on Fi

"Let's get married tomorrow, then I will have you forever." He then moved and said "Ow these bones hurt. I should go and see my osteopath again."

"Oh that reminds me. I need to tell you about a sex crazed osteopath. Plenty of interested men in that field too.

"Maz isn't the exception where men are concerned Fi. You expect too much"

"No. If you want to marry me do not want anyone else. Don't marry if you want to play the field. This particular osteopath was struck off because he was reported by his wife. Don't bother to go to an osteopath tomorrow. Let's see whether I can help"

"Ah bone sex with a difference Fi."

"I've got a book on massage techniques. The correct time to try it out."

"What about your book on the Kama Sutra?"

"We can try that out after we are married."

10.   BONE SEX

"Thanks for the sensation Fi. It was nice having you on top of me even if it was only for a massage"

They were lying together in his bed after Fi had worked on him for over an hour using an ayurvedic balm and her palms to massage him.

"Your patients don't know what they are missing."

"Health care professionals are not supposed to touch inappropriately Yvan. Even in the most intimate of examinations; nor should they talk or text inappropriately.

"Does that apply to any health care professional?"

"Yes. Doctor, nurse, physiotherapist, osteopath."

"I saw an article in Punchng.com about Dr. Nicholas Salway an osteopath. I'll look it up for you"

The General Osteopathic Council has been told how a doctor filmed having sex with his patients in his treatment rooms. A witness narrated how the doctor of osteopathy sent suggestive messages to her.

The messages, which were sent at various times, included: "Just working...I'm a doctor xx give me a minute or two xx." "I'd love to have an inappropriate consultation with you as a 'patient;'" and "I'm an osteopathic doctor...You could come to my college for a thorough examination."

"What does an osteopath do?"

"An osteopathic doctor treats people who are sick or in pain by pushing and moving bones and muscles."

"Not a masseur?"

"No; different."

He also had sex with a female patient in his consultation room while still treating the patient, her husband and their children; and exchanged sexually explicit text messages about a patient with another osteopath.

He made arrangements to meet a woman at the British School of Osteopathy for what he called "adult fun;" while he also sent a text to another osteopath boasting about having had sex with the woman before treating her husband the next day.

Prosecutors said they could provide evidence of "inappropriate consultations" as his efforts were "sexually motivated" which "transgressed sexual boundaries and/or professional boundaries,"

The General Council of Osteopathy decided that Salway had crossed the "unacceptable professional conduct" threshold because he had clearly violated Osteopathic Practice Standards.

After a nine-month suspension order the Council eventually ruled that he could no longer practice because the claims he faced were so serious.

The committee said: "The registrant consciously and deliberately blurred the boundaries between his professional life and personal life.

"If I'd met you as a patient Yvan I would be very professional and we would never be here together.

"Didn't you get into trouble for going to a patient's house?"

"Yes although the General Medical council were idiots in that regard. If you go to a patients house to do good and not abuse or take advantage of patients then they should be applauding you. My problem was I was not apologetic to the Council and did not say I was sorry. In fact I was proud of what I did because I was trying to save patients"

"Yes I saw that chapter in your book "Murder in Medicine"

"Do gynaecologists get into trouble? Sticking their fingers where they shouldn't?"

"Depends on why they are doing it. I'll tell you about it later. We should get up and show something for the day. Lying around without productivity drives me crazy.

He laughed. "Since I am irresistibly drawn to your loins, I'm always ready to produce with you if that's what you want."

"I'm past procreation Yvan. I have 3 beautiful, successful children I do not need any more but you should worry about the spying wife. If you have anything to hide don't marry me."

11. **WIFE SPY**

Dr Christopher Ball-Nossa was given a two-year community order at Warwick Crown Court in January after admitting six charges of making indecent images of children.

The Medical Practitioners Tribunal Service has ruled he be erased from the General Medical Council register because there remained a risk of "repetition" of the offence.

At the time of his arrest in June 2018, Ball-Nossa was working at University Hospital Coventry.

His sentencing hearing in court in January was told the 35-year-old's wife had raised concerns to police about material she found on his laptop when she borrowed it.

Police found 1,520 indecent images and movies on his laptop with some being category A, the most serious of images, the hearing was told she had found similar images almost a decade ago, which he dismissed as "pop-ups".

It said a copy of his pre-sentence report revealed he admitted to having "inappropriate thoughts" from the age of 17.

"That is the reason he did medicine" Yvan said. "Not to save lives."

"Yes. Don't trust me I'm a doctor should be the caveat to any consultation."

"Patients do not realise that the title does not come with an automatic clearance."

"Caveat emptor"

"Yes but patients beware rather than buyer"

The panel dismissed Ball-Nossa's claims he viewed the images not for "sexual gratification" but as a way to "calm himself", adding he had given no evidence of how he would avoid viewing them in future stressful situations.

Although rehabilitation requirements were imposed as part of his sentence, remediation will be a "long and hard process" so there remains a "risk of repetition", it added.

Ball-Nossa was previously ordered to register as a sex offender for 10 years and made subject to a sexual harm prevention order for the same period.

12.   GYNAE SEX

"We should talk softly if you want to hear more. I can hear Maria scraping the skin off the potatoes. She is preparing for lunch. Does she know I stay overnight in my own bedroom?"

"I think that she thinks you pretend to be virtuous. Sometimes your hair is in my bed."

"Not my pubic ones though"

"I don't think she scrutinizes in that type of detail or rifles through the rubbish hunting for condoms"

"The only advantage of sleeping with an old woman is that you don't need a condom."

Yvan shouted out "Maria when you have a moment can we have tea?"

Fi jumped up "Yvan she is busy. I'll get it."

"And can I have a biscuit as well?"

Fi returned with the tea and the Amaretti di saronno biscuits.

 Dipping her biscuits in the tea she said "I asked my friend who is a gynaecologist why he chose the speciality"

"What did he say?"

"He said that there was a limited amount of disease to study so you could be good at it. You'd know everything"

Yvan looked at her with disapproval. "That's not the answer I expected."

"I believed him. Did you want me to say it was because they'd be looking at your privates? Sticking fingers into you and generally having a good time? Some do"

"More like what I imagined Fi" Yvan said "More. Let's have it. Who have you got in mind?"

Manish Shah cited the high-profile health cases of celebrities Angelina Jolie and Jade Goody to talk his victims, who were aged from 15 to 39, into agreeing to the medical checks.

The 50-year-old, who claimed he had been practising "defensive medicine", flouted medical guidelines by giving healthy women under 25 smear tests and by making breast examinations on under-50s.

Shah, who will serve a minimum of 15 years behind bars, preyed on many of the women because of their ages or family history of cancer. He did not always wear gloves to carry out checks and in one case left a woman entirely naked on an examination table, the Old Bailey heard. Shah also breached guidelines on the use of chaperones during intimate examinations.

He was found guilty of 25 sexual offences against six victims at Mawney medical centre, in Romford, east London, between 2009 and 2013. He was also convicted of offences relating to 18 other women at an earlier trial. In total he committed 90 sexual assaults on 24 female patients whom he persuaded to undergo unnecessary intimate examinations for his own gratification

He was labelled a "master of deception" by the judge as he was handed three life sentences.

"If someone approaches you to do a vaginal examination without wearing gloves all you have to do is say "Put them on, or you are not doing it to me.

"And if you've got a sore throat you say "'You're examining the wrong end doc." Yvan winked at her as he said it

"I'm being serious Yvan. Patients need a chaperone and can refuse anything a doctor suggests and they can change their doctor"

"Sorry Fi. That was unhelpful but you are much too serious about the whole business."

"If a doctor does something to a patient without their consent they are committing assault. I really dislike the medical profession."

"At these hearings do they ask for an explanation of behaviour?"

"Of course but they didn't accept his."

"What if he is the only doctor in the practice?"

"Change the practice. But sometimes you are stuck. That's what happens to University Students. University doctors are usually single handed so they can't change."

"Can a doctor refuse to see a patient?"

"Doctors have the right to remove a patient from a GP practice list. This should be a rare event. Reasons include: disagreement between the practice and patient, and an irretrievable breakdown of the relationship or that the patient has died or moved outside the practice area"

"Can patients change their doctors?"

"Patients have a right to change their practice but University students find it easier to go to the campus doctor."

Yvan was grinning

"What?" Fi said surprised at his expression

"Just thinking of all those young women."

"Banish that thought Yvan. It ill behoves you."

"Not for me; for the doctor. Delectable females in skimpy attire."

"The most famous perverted gynaecologist was George Tyndall. He had a large population of young females to abuse In his 27 years at the University of Southern California's student health clinic.

These allegations of serial misconduct by the gynaecologist have affected a generation of alumnae. In the wake of a Times report detailing three decades of complaints against Tyndall, more than 400 people contacted a USC hotline. The accusations against Tyndall date to the early 1990s and include reports that he photographed patients' genitals, touched women inappropriately during pelvic exams and made suggestive and sometimes crude remarks about their bodies.

"What was his defence?"

"In a letter to the Times newspaper, he said, "Patients sometimes fabricate stories.""

"All 400 of them?"

"Amazing that he thinks anyone will believe that explanation" Yvan's grin was wider. "He suffered from a 27 year itch which he wanted to scratch all the time."

The Times interviewed more than two dozen alumnae and former clinic employees, many of whom spoke on the condition of anonymity. Their experiences span three decades and vary widely. Some women said they felt Tyndall's exams were inappropriate and complained immediately.

"How did they do so?"

The grin had disappeared from Yvan's face and was replaced by anger. The questions came out with the speed of bullets. "How did he get found out? Who came forward? Did he have a chaperone?"

"The chaperone reported him."

Anita Thornton frequently chaperoned for Tyndall as a medical assistant at the student health clinic from 1991 to 2010. "I said I don't want to work with him"

She has trouble maintaining her composure as she recalled the "disgusting" physician.

"I've been holding onto this for many years, and I just get choked up thinking about it," she said. "The man is sick."

Thornton said she found a number of his practices inappropriate — and different from how other gynaecologists worked.

She said that during breast exams, Tyndall would squeeze the patients' breasts tightly and say he wanted to see if any liquid would come out. At the start of the pelvic exams, she said, he put his fingers inside the patients, then stood up and "played" inside their bodies. She said she saw that "every day."

He did rectal exams on some women and she recalled hearing him once comment that "black women have tight butt muscles."

Medical assistants complained to management about a ceiling-high curtain that Tyndall would put between the chaperones and the exam table that shielded what he was doing. Sometimes, Thornton said, he had already begun the pelvic exam before she got to the room.

Tyndall has said he used the curtain to obscure the view into the room through a large window.

In the mid-1990s, Thornton was one of the chaperones who reported Tyndall's photographing of patients' genitals. She said he had three cameras in his office — a colposcopy machine, another that looked like a Polaroid, and a black camera he kept locked in a cabinet: "It was like a professional Canon-type camera with a lens on it."

When The Times newspaper questioned Tyndall he said he had two cameras and used them for legitimate medical reasons.

Tyndall stapled some photos in patients' charts and put others in a box under his desk. When the assistant asked him why he was taking photos, he replied, "I'm going to do some research on the girls."

"I reported him because it was not right how he treated the girls," she said.

"You need to read all the witnesses accounts on the internet Yvan if you want to. As a woman and a doctor I really don't want to talk about them because I get frustrated at the thought that this man perpetrated abuse for 27 years.

"Maybe the ruling should be that University doctors should be female?"

"I think so or at least have two people; one a woman. More importantly as I said in my book 'Murder in Medicine'. These girls should know their rights and refuse the exam or the doctor."

"They can't afford to go off campus though can they?"

"That I think was the problem and the reason his abuse carried on for so long."

"One of them who graduated to be a lawyer sued him."

"Notoriety. Fi. He earned himself a place on Wikipedia and cost the University millions."

"Wikipedia? Tell me what it says."

The accusations of George Tyndall have become the largest investigation of sexual abuse performed by LAPD against a single perpetrator. After the discovery of illicit photos in Tyndall's office, LAPD obtained half a dozen search warrants for his personal property including Tyndall's home and storage units. Findings included hundreds more images of unclothed women, some taken in clinic settings. Dozens of hard drives were also discovered and are still undergoing review. Since the searches of Tyndall's belongings it has been discovered that he was selling "homemade sex tapes" and photos in the Philippines.

In June 2019 USC agreed to a $215 million class-action settlement for tens of thousands of women treated by Tyndall from August 14, 1989-June 21,2016. Amounts vary from $2,500 to $250,000 and will be compensated based on the severity of misconduct and the patient's willingness to provide written statements or interviews with mental health professionals.

George Tyndall was married to Daisy Patricio, a Filipina woman from Mindanao. He was approximately 20 years her senior. They lived in the Lafayette Park neighbourhood of Los Angeles and did not have any children. I'm not sure whose idea it was to sell his home video's in the Phillipines his or hers"

"The University should have actioned the outrage earlier, without letting his passion and perversions go unfettered for years ." Yvans gaze dipped hungrily to Fi's breasts. "Could I examine you?" Fi gave him a sardonic look. Then laughed as she saw his disgruntled countenance

"I guess the gay guys on campus were ok."

"With Tyndall yes they would have been, but not if they got a pervert gay doctor. He could suggest that rectal exams or intimate genital examinations be performed. I haven't heard of such as yet."

"We'll be late if we sit here discoursing on sexuality Fi. We need to get to the evening bridge game. Tell me more later."

13.   **GAY SEX**

They were sitting at the bar drinking after the evening bridge game when Renee joined them.

"You both did well tonight Fi. Sixty percent. What's the story today? I'm bored and don't want to go back to my cold and lonely flat."

Yvan said "I've just opened this bottle of Cabernet Sauvignon Renee. Join me as Fi doesn't drink C2H5OH."

"Sure. Go on Fi, oh wise and witty scribe; tell us about Pervert spotting in Medicine."

"Thomas Jenkins, a 28 year old junior doctor logged onto gay dating app Grindr and asked another user Liam, who he thought was 13, for sex. He was caught by an undercover police officer.

"It's not a patient" Renee said

"No but doctors are not allowed to have heinous thoughts or actions"

"Like priests?" Yvan flashed her a grin.

"Yes. Although priests are pretty perverted. No sexually inappropriate advents into any sphere for doctors. He was urging a 13-year-old boy on Grindr to have unprotected sex with him.

"What was the story? How was he such an idiot?"

The junior doctor, from Manchester, went on a wild night out after completing a hospital night shift during which he drank and took Mephedrone at the party.

He then brought a man back to his home for intercourse before abusing more drugs. Shortly afterwards he went on Grindr where he made contact with the boy, known as 'Liam14' and sent the obscene pictures of himself.

He sent further obscene pictures of himself over a two-day period, asking the boy how he lost his virginity and 'how do you like to be f****d?'"

"In messages to the boy, Jenkins said he 'wanted to slap him about a bit' during intercourse." Remind me to tell you about sadomasochism at some point Yvan."

"Thomas thought he was attempting to groom an underage boy, but it was the police officer. He was arrested at Wrexham Maelor Hospital where he was doing the second year of a foundation course in psychiatry.

He admitted inciting the boy of 13 to engage in sexual activity at Manchester Crown Court. Jenkins qualified as a doctor at Cardiff University two years before his arrest. He started a conversation with Liam and exchanged sexually explicit messages and pictures and asked to meet him in person for sex.

Renee said "My gay friend Rodd showed me some of the pictures on Grindr. Men showing open holes and big bananas sometimes with no faces. Rodd recognised one of his friends by the pointed shoes below his dong"

Yvan twinkled at her "I thought you were going to say by his bananas and oranges Renee"

"Probably the fruit bowl pictures that Jenkins sent to "Liam 14". At the time Jenkins was living in Manchester which I think has the next biggest gay population after London.   My friend said her gay ex-husband would frequently take an afternoon trip to Manchester which she thinks was for gay sex."

"Why did she think that?"

"He was extremely abusive to her on his return from Manchester. He tried to pick a fight about useless things like the colour of new bedroom curtains."

"Odd. You would think he'd be soothed by his interaction"

"His conscience pricked him. He wanted to try and make her feel she was the bad party so he could feel better about himself."

Jenkins, whose evidence was deemed "open and honest", spoke of his passion for being a doctor and claimed the grooming was "out of character".

He asked to be suspended from the medical register and said he had taken "steps on the road of remediation".

"Jenkins hearing was in Manchester Fi wasn't it? He shamed himself where he lived." Renee straightened her tartan jacket "What happened to him?

A judge ordered him to take part in a sex offenders' programme for three years and he was placed on the sex offenders register for five years.

 "He was struck off the medical register of the General Medical Council and will never be able to work in this country as a doctor.

The tribunal panel agreed Jenkins had brought the medical profession into disrepute and fellow doctors would find his actions deplorable.

"Has anyone ever done a follow up article on these doctors? What becomes of them? Can they go somewhere else and practice medicine?"

"Thomas Jenkins could Renee. He will have his certificate of graduation and a sign off after 1 year in psychiatry. He could turn up in another country say he has stopped paying registration fees to the GMC and if they didn't bother to check the GMC register, another country could employ him."

"Do gays prey on their hospital patients?"

"Myles Bradbury certainly did. They have their sexuality in overdrive"

"Yes. I love Rodd, my gay friend but the stories he tells me are amazing. Have you heard about Chem sex Fi?"

"No. What is that?"

"Sex with Viagra Fi. Another glass of wine Renee? Wet your whistle for this educational 'tour de force'."

"Thanks Yvan. I will; don't want it to go to waste. No. Not sex with Viagra

He filled up their wine glasses with a steady right hand pushing the edge of the glass to the wall to steady it and prevent any spillage.

14.   CHEM SEX

Sipping her glass of Cabernet Sauvignon and eating the drying pieces of chicken that she had failed to eat while listening to Fi. Renee remembered what Rodd had told her

'Chemsex' is a vernacular term used to describe group sexual encounters between gay and bisexual men.'

"Orgies? It's outlandish"

"Yes group sex in which the recreational drugs GHB/GBL, mephedrone and crystallised methamphetamine are consumed."

"Did you participate Rodd?" Renee was looking shocked

"Yes In Manchester in 2011" He looked furtively embarrassed.

"At the time reports of chemsex to Britain's National Health Service (NHS) reached a sufficiently high number that it began to develop treatment strategies targeted specifically at chemsex related health problems. At the end of 2015 there was a moral panic about the problems chemsex posed for gay and bisexual men and I stopped."

"You could have contracted AIDS Rodd"

 "Yes that was one of the reasons for stopping. I also met Norman and I developed a different sort of relationship. No more orgies. By then Chemsex had emerged as a distinct cultural practice in the UK, specifically in London."

"I don't even do postcode lottery sex anymore"

"What's that Rodd?"

"When gays are in a relationship that is not exclusive and committed they have sexual encounters but never within their own postcode area"

"So if you are TW9 which is Kew Gardens, you won't have sex with TW10 which is Richmond?" Renee questioned

"No no. The whole TW area is out but I'd easily have sex in W1 Soho"

"You'd have to carry a London map in your back pocket just to check before you indulge" said Renee laughing

"After 6 years of a committed relationship with Norman and maybe because I have grown older, my longings for those highs are just a dull ache. I used to have a nice little set up. I lined up all the nights in Soho after work identifying the cruising gay guys on Compton Street and in Neal's yard. And weekends there were the orgies in Manchester." His agony at loss of his lifestyle showed.

"Blissful life ruined by Norman."

"You didn't mean that Rodd"

"No I love him; I'm just an old married faggot now."

"Your relationship is the nicest relationship I've seen Rodd; realistic and different. If you say one more negative word I shall report back to Norman."

"Yes. He is a darling. He looks after me but the highs from Chem sex. Don't remind me Renee. I was extremely glamorous and at the orgies I could just wink and they'd come running." Rodd sighed" Chemsex is primarily self-destructive for the gay and bisexual men who practice it. Feral real-time behaviour like that tells a nightmarish story of everyday annihilation."

"Like lemmings killing themselves?"

He turned towards her sadly

"Give me your bosom cuddle Renee. Norman doesn't have any and I'm back to missing my mother again" Renee silently hugged him to her double D cup. His face nestled comfortably. He was silent

15.   DISABLED SEX

"Is your bottom line that you shouldn't trust doctors? Even sexually? You said that in your book 'Murder in Medicine' Yvan's face had fallen.

"Sexually, as well as with your life. That is my feeling. They appear to be smart people who at any point can change. The more I research this the more disgusted I get."

"The worm has turned."

"Sometimes it hasn't turned. It's just appeared over ground squirming and wriggling whereas it was always there underground. They work in their best interests not yours."   Yvan was struggling up the three steps to the front door of his house

"You need to advance plan and adjust this house for a wheelchair which you may need eventually"

"When I'm disabled we can move to a bungalow. I don't want 18th century buildings destroyed."

Maria let them in when Yvan rang the door bell. She had her overcoat on and was ready to leave.

"Have you left dinner on the table?" Yvan asked pompously"

When she had gone and they were eating Fi commented "One day she will say to you "No your dinner is in the dog"

Yvan started laughing. "I don't have a dog. I usually don't act like that. It's you. You make me feel embarrassed at having a girlfriend. I treat her much more 'sympatico' when you aren't around. "

"She doesn't keep track of your sex life Yvan"

"Or lack of it" Yvan said looking at Fi disconsolately.

"Would you stay with me if I was disabled and we weren't married?"

"Need you ask Yvan? I would never leave you like Theepa did Vittorio nor take advantage of you. Not like those sex mad doctors taking advantage of their disabled and vulnerable patients."

"Which one are you talking about now?"

"Steven Ashenford a GP in Telford persuaded a teenage acne patient with learning difficulties to perform a sex act on him at his surgery.

"What do you do to get someone to perform a sex act on you? I'll use the technique on you Fi"

"I'm not 17 or sexually naive Yvan and you and I have a lot of safe sex encounters including oral sex. That's why you are still around. If you are a doctor, you abuse your position of trust to gain gratification in a "most reprehensible way" with a 17-year-old girl who doesn't know any better."

Dr Ashenford struck up a friendship with the girl during appointments at the Sutton Hill Medical Practice to treat her acne and a bad back.

During one consultation in March 2007 he touched her breasts and remarked "that was nice". A week later he told her to remove her top and perform oral sex on him at the surgery.

"Did he admit? Was there any evidence?"

Dr Ashenford denied any sexual relationship with the girl, but admitted at the hearing he had sex with two other patients while working at Oakengates Medical Practice one year before that and at Sutton Hill practice a year later.

The GP had also struck up a friendship with an 11-year-old girl when he worked at the Princess Royal Hospital in Telford, sending her 10 text messages a day and making social plans with her mother.

"Who was he targeting?"

"Probably the girl because older women wouldn't be laying out that easily"

"I know that to my cost" Yvan said "although you are the loveliest of things to hold in my arms."

"You thought you were playing with fire when you approached me and all you got were embers Yvan. Ashenford doesn't know what a professional boundary is"

"Anyone knows you shouldn't have oral sex with a patient in the surgery" Yvan's voice was gruff.

"Yes relationships with patients are taboo."

"Was he just frustrated?"

"He was married to an older Russian woman and they had a daughter who was brain damaged at birth so he could have had sex at home. All the Russians I've seen are attractive although the Russian man I overheard through my bedroom wall wasn't a stayer. Came quickly."

"Russians are always blamed" Yvan said referring to his Russian heritage. "You won't have that problem with me I can assure you. I hope they struck Ashenford off the medical register."

"Yes and they did the same to the Chancellor, George Osborne's, younger brother Adam Osborne for having sex with a vulnerable patient. Adam was five years younger than the chancellor.

"Yes I saw that newspaper report. George was chancellor at the time in 2008. Adam was an idiot. With all his prestigious connections he would have been able to get any female. Why go for a vulnerable patient?"

"He was married Yvan and obviously horny and not able to have 'no-ties' sex."

"I'd forgotten that he was married. I remember he had been treating the patient at a private practice in central London for depression, anxiety and chronic fatigue."

"Yes for nearly 4 years; February 2011 to late 2014.

"Why did he split up with her?"

"Found greener pastures I guess. He ended the affair by email. And the mother-of-two tried to commit suicide and then reported him to the General Medical Council."

"That is what any doctor who has sex with a patient should be afraid of. A report to the GMC. They can lose their livelihood for it. Is it worth the orgasmic moments?"

"I'm waiting to give up my freedom to have sex with you Fi"

"When Adam found out what had happened despite knowing of her fragile state and suicide attempt, he bombarded her with threatening emails over a 10-day period begging her to retract her complaint.

He told her "I will make sure you pay"

"She had him over a barrel" Yvan said coldly "Don't like women like that"

"He was at fault Yvan. He just got what was coming. Adam pleaded with her to retract saying: "You still have the power to tell the GMC that you made this up because you were angry at me for discontinuing therapy or that you were confused, paranoid, deluded - whatever excuse you can think of."

"Never put anything in writing. It will come to light and haunt you." Yvan was laughing." I guess she showed all that to the GMC?"

"He didn't subscribe to your stratagem Yvan. Yes it all came out"

He also told her: "If I get into trouble for this then I will never forgive you for this and I will make sure you pay."

Another email read: "Please don't do this to me, it will destroy me and my family in public."

"He should have thought of that in the first place stupid f.ck. It wasn't a temporary whim. Four years of using her"

Following the split, the woman told him: "I'm very much balancing on the edge and it's so easy for me to tip over just now."

"Did his wife know?"

"Not sure whether Adams wife knew before or after. All the newspapers say is that she did know. To quote, "Dr Osborne's wife had knowledge of the woman.""

"Another idiot who loses his job, livelihood money and career for sex"

"Disgraced his family too; George's political career went after that"

"Here's a new spin on it Fi. He did it to get himself the publicity he always wanted and usurp his famous brother. Or was it out of jealousy?"

"Traded financial security and fulfilment for a moment of fame or wanting to get back?" Yvan was walking round the dining table as he talked.

"No. Just reckless and think they won't be found out. People don't give up their comfort zone that easily if they think they will be found out."

Having reached her, he stooped and silenced her further words with a kiss, his tongue lingering longingly.

16.   CAMERA SEX

Yvan lifted his chin, refusing to be judged for his behaviour and yet wanting to come clean

"You and I are a single entity Fi. We've been together 2 years now. I have to tell you what I did"

Fi sat down on the sofa with some trepidation not knowing what was coming. She made light of it. "Because of your unfulfilled passion you've had sex with Maria" Yvan looked amused "Never"

"You've been to a prostitute last night when I was at Renee's house."

"No Mama's ruler treatment put me off that."

"You've been photographing me in the shower without my knowledge?"

"You've let me photograph you in the shower. Why should I be doing it secretly?"

"What then? You don't do drugs, phone sex or anything vaguely worthy of mentioning so what is it?"

"I spent hours last night reading all George Tyndall's case and I got turned on by it. Boner material and emissions were the order of the day."

Fi's mirth and laughter continued for a full minute. She doubled over. When she stopped her stomach muscles hurt from the peals of raucous laughter that had left her. Her mirth was added to by relief when she heard the harmless announcement. Towards the end of her laughing Yvan had joined in. She laughed so hard tears rolled out of her eyes.

"Ok Yvan. Your punishment is to recount all the stories about Tyndall as one sexual narrative and see whether I will get turned on by it.

"Lots of breast squeezing, vaginal and rectal fingering and inappropriate comments together with photographic images" Yvan said

"That is not good enough Yvan. I want it told as a story. Try. Tell it like I told Theepa's story. Pretend. It's a good exercise for you and you may even end up writing your story of the holocaust and your near escape from Auschwitz. If you are good at narrative you may write your own book at some point in the future."

Yvan's voice faltered as he started and then grew stronger as he got into the character acting role.

 Dr. George Tyndall treated tens of thousands of patients he called "Trojan women."

Fi interrupted "Yes I saw that term. The newspaper never gave an explanation for it."

"I think the Greek Trojan horse had lots hidden inside it which only came to light when it was undone like Tyndall's patients disrobing I guess revealing themselves."

Fi said "I was waiting for a deeply disturbing revelation and all I got was a boner- wanking incident. Your story had better be good."

"Do you want parallel narratives or shall I handle dozens of characters in one?"

"Whatever gets the male sexual adventurer aroused."

Tyndall is sitting in his room waiting for his next appointment.

Diana Bohan walks in to the student health clinic. It is the fall of 1992 but it has been signalled by warm weather.

She wears typical student attire. T shirt, a short denim skirt and 'Vans' on her feet.

"I've got tenderness in my hips Dr Tyndall."

"What are you studying Diana?"

"I'm an architecture student."

"How old are you?

"25. It may be nothing. I walked a lot on my summer trip to Europe and probably have bruised myself"

 A pelvic exam is necessary, to see "structural problems" within." Tyndall says

Diana thinks "This is kind of weird because I'm not here for this type of appointment,"

An assistant stands by, so Diana takes off her –panties gets up on the couch and spreads her legs.

Tyndall puts his gloves on and approaches her

She lies there thinking 'this is not professional.'

Tyndall says to Diana after he finishes and takes a long time mopping the lubricant off her front and back parts. "I detected nothing unusual. Let's prescribe a physical therapy course. Come back and see me after you've finished."

Diana does not go back.

"She is thinking, 'Wow, I had to get through a pelvic exam just to get to this," She did not tell anyone about the format of the appointment but is thinking

Years later she thinks 'Maybe I should call US Campus and see if he has done this to anyone else?"

"Yvan that did not turn me on one bit. You'll have to try harder"

"Can I tell you the story of another girl?. I'll think of someone sexier."

"Ok second chance. Three strikes and you are out"

Chelsea Wu is 19 She is naive having never been to a doctor without her parents by her side. She has never seen a gynaecologist. Being young, she doesn't have a framework for what is acceptable."

"Come in Chelsea. I'm Dr Tyndall My wife is Chinese."

Chelsea is reassured by this information. Her respectful Asian background makes her blindly trusting of doctors. Tyndall asks prying questions about her sex life, showed an unsettling interest in her Chinese heritage.

 He rapid fires a series of questions,

"How many sexual partners have you had? Did you enjoy it? You can decline to reply at any time."

Chelsea answers

"I need to do a pelvic exam Chelsea"

He gets his gloves out whilst she jumps onto the examination couch. She has a shift-dress on which she lifts up pulling off her panties.

Tyndall while putting his fingers inside her says. "You have a very muscular canal," he said. "You must be a runner."

They return to his office after the pelvic exam.

Tyndall asks her to sit next to him at his desk. He quizzes her about her heritage.

"I've lived in China and the U.S. doctor."

"Many Chinese patients come to me not knowing much about sex. They all love me,"

Chelsea walks away thinking "I don't understand all this interest in China. It took 15 or 20 minutes, longer than my pelvic exam." Tyndall is "odd" but maybe he is a "well meaning" physician.

"Why was my first instinct to leave?

"Is that it Yvan?

"Yes. Why? Did I fail again?

"Third time lucky. Try again

"Ok Fi Here we go. Let me give her a name"

"Maybe without a name you'll do better? Just say former USC student?

George Tyndall is sitting at his desk. His trouser fronts uplift many times as he thinks about his previous patients. His next student will arrive shortly. Brenda walks in.

She was warned as a freshman in 1990 that Tyndall was known for "always doing a rectal exam."

"I'll just have to grin and bear it to get the prescription" She wants to see the clinic's only full-time gynaecologist Tyndall

The clinical appointment begins innocently enough with Tyndall discussing things that any other doctor would discuss.

"When I went in, I was wary," said Brenda recounting the story to a friend, now a Los Angeles lawyer.

"It wasn't my first pelvic exam" she said "But he was weird, creepy,"

"On the bed Brenda let's see what it is all about."

Brenda knows this is coming and has washed and worn her service knickers for it."

"I wasn't certain what he'd do next. When he initiated a rectal exam, I sat "straight up" and told him it was not necessary."

"He didn't argue with me,"

Tyndall's preference for rectal exams became a running joke among students.

Fi was curious. "I didn't see that part when I reviewed his cases. I thought he was just vaginally obsessed."

The Times newspaper asked him about doing rectal exams. But he did not respond.

Brenda said to The Times "It was always this creep factor" She shuddered.

"At first, I didn't know what was appropriate during a pelvic exam. I had   attended USC as both an undergraduate and law student.

Tyndall routinely inserted his fingers in my vagina, often twice a visit. He required me to fully disrobe so he could conduct breast exams, and always commented on the attractiveness of my breasts, slender body and Asian background.

I had to see Tyndall three times or more in some of my seven years at USC and grew increasingly uncomfortable with each appointment. When I finally asked if I could see a female doctor instead, the clinic told me no one was available.

After The Times' spoke to me I realized how abnormal Tyndall's behaviour was.

"He'd stick his fingers inside me pretty much every time. It was always this creep factor.... He'd check me twice. He'd stick his fingers up there and then we'd talk and he'd say, 'Let me check again. "

During breast exams, he would comment on her figure, she said, and would also tell her that his wife was Asian and petite like her.

"He would squeeze my nipples," she said. "He'd tell me, 'You have nice full breasts' ... 'Not every Asian has nice big breasts.'"

"In hindsight" she said, "I probably should have complained."

Fi said "I commend your professionalism Yvan but I'm sorry to say you have failed your examination as a story teller; certainly not an erotic one. You will make a good docu-journalist though if that's the best you can do. But how could you get horny on those stories? He sounds like a vile pig to me. It's chilling to know, it happened to so many women and that he had the opportunity to have full rein of control even with an assistant in the room."

"I challenge you Fi. You look up one of the stories about him and tell it to me in erotic form"

"I always accept the gauntlet when it is thrown down Yvan."

"I'll have this story in bed Fi. Let's go upstairs. They started mounting the sweeping circular staircase. Yvan stopped and said "Shouldn't they have questioned the fact that the centre's gynaecologist was a man?"

"Unfortunately you couldn't reverse-gender, role-discriminate for the post. Interviewees for a job have to be appointed on ability not gender."

"It's the university's fault Fi; they should have done something about it. Why didn't they? Didn't one of the students sue? She should have filed against Tyndall and the campus."

"I don't know the outcome yet but I hope you are not becoming an old pervert Yvan with all these stories"

"It's harmless Fi. Masturbation. Men do it all the time. More when they are in steady relationships which have got stale sexually. Remember what Woody Allen said "Don't knock masturbation.; it's sex with someone you love" After they both laughed Fi said

"I know. My Scientologist ex-boyfriend said that men masturbate even when they had girlfriends. I was shocked. Now I know that is a fact throughout the whole species I am not concerned"

"The Musician Scientologist?"

"Yes."

"Was the sex great with him?"

"Yes. Loved going down on a woman. Wanted to please."

"Wait till you experience the full me Fi, those events will be wiped out."

Fi stared into the darkened room and the dimmed light visible through the chinks in the bedroom door frame. Yvan always left the chandelier light on in the hallway. She snuggled closer to Yvan smelling his eau de cologne.

"Nudge me if I fall asleep while creating my fictionalised version of Georgie boy."

Georgie boy is driving home from work. His fly is unzipped. He drives an automatic Chrysler with power-assisted steering. He is thinking back to the three students he saw that day and savouring the intimacy that he had. He strokes himself.

Wuhan Liu's breasts were magnificent. 'She believed my explanation of how to do a breast self-exam.' He smiles to himself.

When I described to her how she should be in the shower and should be wet and covered in soap suds I nearly came myself. I would have loved to have been in the shower with her rubbing my hands over those gorgeous breasts.

Wuhan would feel the press of my erection hard against her stomach. She is awkward and shy having only had one boyfriend before. Georgie imagines lifting her and pushing her onto his firmness; moving her up and down on it until he gets glorious release.

Georgie is stopped at a traffic light. He covers his exposed groin with a newspaper in case the 4x4 beside him sees his erection. 'Would she think it's length was too much? Lot's of him was still out when he had sex with his wife. Wuhan would feel so tight when he enters her but soon becomes slippery with the secretions.

He thinks of the next student, the bisexual lesbian Maggie. 'I would love to go with her to a sex shop. We'd buy the lesbian movies. Some with girls and men together. I suggested a sex shop she should visit but together she may even let me help her choose from the different kinds of dildos that she might be able to get. I would emphasize the ones that look more human' more realistic looking. The 'veiny', kind"

I would use it on her with my hand massaging her and when she is near release it would be my flesh in the sticky honey pot. She would be enticed to having sexual encounters with both men and women not just women.

Georgie boy remembers his conversation with her. She has not had penetrative sex with a man. "Oh, so you're a virgin,"

When Maggie objects to the label, he says, "But let's be real. No penis, no sex."

He squeezes her breasts roughly, calling them "lovely and very symmetrical. And says as he he inserts his fingers inside her "I bet you're pretty used to this."

His eyes glaze over he wishes he can place her on his member. His demeanour changes   in the car as his rhythmical movements continue.

He arrives at his home near ejaculating. His wife greets him in the hall.

"He lifts her dress pins her to the wall and within a few thrusts he comes. She feels happy not realising what has whet his appetite. She has cooked a nice Filipino meal which they eat together. Crispy pata, Chicken inasal, Taba ng talangka.

After dinner she goes to bed.

Later Georgie boy goes to his study. He thinks of the incident with Veroni, the pretty law student. He takes the photo's out of his briefcase. His trousers tent. He is pointing upwards.

"Anita" he had said to the chaperone "go get a speculum."

"It's in the drawer in the instrument cabinet"

"No I looked for it; it isn't there." Georgie insists

"Have you checked the drawer in the exam room?"

"I did. It wasn't." They argued for a few minutes before Anita leaves.

Within five seconds of her leaving the room, he 'finds' the speculum. Veroni thinks 'That's odd.

Take off your dress and underwear"

"She lies fully naked on the couch taking off her spotted dress and matching underwear.

"He is playing around with her with his fingers. He does not use the speculum. The famous rectal examination occurs." Just as he concludes Anita returns with the speculum.

Yvan says "Yes I am sexually aroused by your stories. I remember that one."

Getting into the mood of the story Yvan says

"After Georgie boy leaves, Anita walks over to Veroni saying, 'You know he's not supposed to perform the exam without me in the room."

Fi continues

 Veroni thinks 'He got her out of the room to finger me."

Yvan is relaxed and amorous. He puts his hand out to Fi's neck and strokes downwards. She lets him play continuing her story. He strokes the points and moves his mouth to them.

 Georgie remembers feeling Trish. Wet, warm and cosy. His fingers inside her he asked 'Are you a runner?'

"Sometimes,' Trish replied.

"Well, your pelvic muscles are really tight; squeeze my fingers." He was moving his fingers from "side to side"

"Did she say something?" Yvan interjected

"She must have thought that there was no oddity as there was a nurse in the room."

Georgie inserts a speculum and removes her IUD which was the reason she has gone to see him. He knows she is lying on the exam table in a fog of pain.

Now back in his study Georgie takes the IUD out and smells it. It is covered in blood and secretions." He plays with himself.

Emotionally charged and with the smell of Veroni on his hands he jumps onto his wife   who is lying in bed half asleep. He spreads her legs. With no preamble he imagines that it is Veroni under him as he rhythmically goes in and out of her.

Yvan groans and moans as he tries to go under Fi's underwear with his paralysed left arm.

"You are a great story teller" he says after obtaining release.

Later he says to FI in his post ejaculate state "You cheated. It was all pretend with a bit of fact thrown in."

 "That is what story telling is all about Yvan. Take a small piece of fact and weave a web of lies around it"

It was Saturday morning. Yvan had lazed about till 10 am and now he was sitting at the breakfast table. Fi had fried eggs and bacon and opened a can of baked beans to which she had added rosemary, chives and flaked chillies

"Stunningly disturbing to the taste buds Fi; that combination."

Fi, warmed by the compliment of her gastronomic creativity said

"But don't get rid of Maria when we marry. She makes great tortia, Spanish omelettes, fritata's and risotto.

"Years of practice on me perfected her art. Talking about practices, are doctors allowed to photograph patients?"

"I've got lots of photos of feet, faces, hands and oddities on my phone Yvan. So long as the patient doesn't mind it is perfectly acceptable but I don't think I've ever photographed intimate places." She thought and said

"No I haven't ever taken any. Most hospitals have photography departments to which you can send patients for a professional photograph."

"I fail to understand the mental dynamic behind abusive images taken by doctors."

"I don't either, but deepening depravity occurs with advancing technology."

"How so?"

"Plenty of ways to spy on people and get images which they are not aware are being taken.

"I've photographed cute children on the tube; and another cute little boy at Kew garden station playing the same riff on his guitar. About 10 chord changes. It was a nice riff so I gave him a pound coin but it was very innocent"

"What lengths people go to, to get these images. I saw an article in the Evening Standard newspaper about this Hospital Manager Ian Newby who was on the London eye filming up the skirts of innocent girls passing by. Did you see that in the Evening Standard?

"Yes I did read that. Wasn't there a police man who did the same? You just can't blame Health care staff alone" Fi's voice faltered then strengthened.

"It's an enigma. Do they choose the hospital as a place of work for that reason? To work in the hope of seeing naked bodies?"

"Mutilayered thrills? Thrill of taking the image and thrill of looking at the images afterwards?"

"Ian Newby may not have chosen his job for that reason. He looked under skirts on the Southbank. He was pretending to tie his shoelaces as he used his mobile phone to take the picture but he was spotted and confronted by the outraged woman. She called the police and they found more than 100 upskirt images and videos on his phone."

"Any at his work?"

"Yes but not of patients. One of his female colleagues at Ashford and St Peters Hospital. He had been collecting these images over a period of 4 years."

"What about his female friends?"

"He had images from a wedding he attended and a scout event."

"Was he married?"

"Married for 12 years"

"I guess the wife didn't know?"

"Do wives ever know what their husbands get up to without being spies?"

"You would if you lived with me."

"You are honest with me about your sexuality but if you wanted to photograph unknown knickers would you tell me?"

"The thought has to come first, then the deed. I am not sure any of my thoughts have been that unusual."

"Did he lose his job?"

"The majority of people who get caught doing this kind of sexually motivated action do. The Judge Susan Green told him he deserved a 14 week prison sentence as it passed the 'custody threshold' but she didn't send him to prison for outraging public decency. She suspended sentence for 1 year and made him pay £1250 in compensation and an £85 victim surcharge. I presume he lost his job."

"The worst of the doctors was a guy who went to great lengths to get images from known and unknown people"

"Who was that? How did he do it?" Yvan staring blankly repeated himself "Have you told me the story before?"

17. **YEOH CAMERA SEX**

"Spying equipment"

 They had now finished the evening bridge game and the three cronies were sitting at the bar in Young Chelsea." Other bridge players were discussing the evening game with hand records of the results but Yvan and Renee preferred to hear Fi's stories.

Dr Lam Hoe Yeoh, was caught finally at age 62. The perverted spy doctor filmed more than 1,000 patients, staff, and visitors using hospital toilets, and labelled the sick videos with titles such as 'Exeter 10/3 mum-young blonde' and 'teenager bum',

"I hope the pervert received a significant and substantial sentence Fi. How did he get discovered?"

"One of his cameras fell from a toilet wall in St. Anthony's Hospital in Cheam prompting officers to search his home, offices, cars and computers. He had filmed himself by mistake when setting up the spying equipment"

"What speciality was he?

"Until his fall from grace he had been one of the country's leading ear doctors. He admitted using his position to plant cameras and film people using the toilets at the Epsom and St Helier Hospital, St Antony's in Cheam, and a clinic in Thames Ditton." Yvan licked the egg yolk dripping from his fork.

"He also had footage from filmed men, women, and children in other unidentified clinics including one in Nottingham."

"He is a psycho sicko. What did he do with them?"

"He admitted to masturbating over some of the videos. His computer showed a woman changing her sanitary towel."

"He really is aberrant. What is sexy about that?" Fi locked her eyes with Yvan.

"Horrified former friends and colleagues packed the public gallery of Croydon Crown Court to hear the doctor admit his twisted behaviour, including hiding cameras in his watch, pens, and lining of bins, to capture lewd footage that he would use to make mini-home movies.

"Sexually immature to not get past the looking stage"

"Accurate analysis Yvan; immaturity. Yeoh was a compulsive collector of Enid Blyton novels although he did have one video with extreme pornography.

"What kind of person was he? Did he have friends?"

"He filmed guests who visited his home in Garratts Lane, Banstead so were they really friends or victims?"

"What a price to pay for a Malaysian Chinese meal."

"What was the extreme pornography?"

"Humans carrying out sex acts on dogs."

"It occurs. Farmers and sheep."

"My dad always said "Perverts exist because erections need a resting place"

"I disagree" Yvan said "Look what I've been doing most of my life. And there are always rubber dolls. Animals cannot give consent. Like your poem they are probably thinking – Why do I want a man in my parts?"

Renee said "Which poem? Which book? Have I missed it?"

"You have Renee. It's on my web page. Buy a copy for your gay friend Rodd. 'Naughty poems for naughty people' available from Amazon.

"Let's go and look round a sex shop in Soho. See what's out there for the single man. Did you want to come Renee?"

"Poor victims and friends."

"Yes more than 1,084 unidentified victims and 30 identified."

"Was he single?"

"No. His wife Ivy Muihong Sng, 57, faced a single charge of voyeurism relating to footage filmed in their home, but the prosecution opted not to pursue the charge."

"What an impact on people who were filmed."

"Peter Clements, prosecuting, said one child was now scared of seeing Yeoh in the street and feared he was hiding in the cupboards, filming her at her new home.

Other former friends and colleagues have had counselling since the voyeurism surfaced, reporting they find it more difficult to trust other staff, and fear they are being filmed whenever they use the toilet.

"Fi I think they have a one way mirror in the toilet in Bathurst Deli. Whenever I use it, I make sure no part of me is exposed. I keep my bum hidden and if I sit on the toilet with my trousers down I switch the light off."

"You've never told me that before?"

"You might have thought I was paranoid."

Renee burst out laughing. "I'll give them a wave and a burlesque act before I pee" She stood up and gave a grind her hips rolling.

The two of them were laughing loudly. Then Yvan became more serious

"It's not a joke Renee. In hotel rooms I always check for spy cameras."

"Yvan you amaze me. Even without knowing about Yeoh?

"What do you do in hotel rooms that you don't want looked at?" Renee leaned forward and nearly fell off the bar stool waiting for the answer.

"Watch graphic movies and have natural outcomes"

"I think lots of people do that sort of thing. But I've had my suspicion about many people through my life with recording equipment including a famous city lawyer who I think had a camera in a clock in his bedroom. This was when I was thin and pretty" Renee sighed

"You had sex with him?"

"Yes after I got divorced he targeted me. He wanted sex and always wanted to have sex at the middle of the bed which is right in the field of vision of his clock."

"He must be over 70 now"

"I guess so"

"Does aberrant and inappropriate sexuality in doctors continue as they get older Fi? Does it get worse?"

"That's an interesting question. I should look up ages of offenders but my off- the-cuff analysis says they are all ages; young to old."

They bid Renee goodbye and headed home.

18.   THE OLD PERVERT

Lying in bed Yvan said. "My sexuality has waned as I got older. Does that happen to the perverted doctors?"

"I think their sexuality gets worse as they get older. No young women are going to look at them as they are probably old fat and greasy so they use patients as their targets. Certainly that was what Georgie boy was doing although he started when he was very young. He had 27 years of fingering under his belt before he was reported."

Yvan nodded jerkily. "I guess you have such cases. Which was the oldest that you can remember?"

"Dr Stanislaw Franciszek Zulichoswki was aged 71 when he carried out a "disgraceful" sexually motivated internal examination of a female patient. The GMC struck him off. He appealed and was struck off the medical register by order of the President of the High Court.

"What are the details? Why did he appeal?"

"Lunacy. The woman in her twenties went for a medical examination and "received anything but", said the judge Mr Justice Peter Kelly so I'm not sure why he bothered to appeal."

The woman said to the judge that when she asked Dr Stanislaw Franciszek Zulichoswki, for an explanation for what he did, he told her he got "carried away"

"Why? Was she in seductive ensemble?"

"It doesn't matter Yvan. If a patient comes for an examination with a thong, sexy knickers and stockings she is still a patient being seen by a doctor. I cannot believe Dr Zulichoswki 's, reply. He said

"Well, I just kind of started liking it and got carried away" before also adding "well, you know I am just a man, not only a doctor."

"Was that just one incident?"

"The Medical Council, following a fitness to practice (FTP) inquiry made several findings of professional misconduct against him and, applied to the High Court to strike him off its specialist register."

"Was he practising in England?"

"Not sure where, but when they cancelled his registration his address was Russell Street, Behan Square, Dublin. He could have been travelling from there to work anywhere in the UK.

"Can you imagine it Fi. I'll tell you the story now"

Yvan started narrating his own version

"Come in Beyonce"

Beyonce is a black Afro carribean model. She glides into the room with her models walk.

Dr. Zulichoswki is bowled over by her beauty.

He stands and bows. "Hello. How are you?"

"I'm Dr Stanislaw Franciszek Zulichoswki. Call me Stan."

"I've got this painful lump doctor. It's on my privates"

Stan's ears perk up as do other parts of his anatomy.

"Take your clothes off my dear. I need to give you a full examination"

Beyonce is accustomed to stripping off in changing rooms on fashion shoots.

Stanislaw doesn't give her any privacy while she does so watching her get undressed.

"He pulls his doctor's white coat over his tenting trousers"

"Do you want my bra off?"

"Yes we need a full examination."

She takes off her leopard skin thong and silk matching leopard skin bra."

"He feels her breasts rubbing his erection back and forth on the side of the examination couch."

"Beyonce is lying there comfortable and relaxed at the touch.

"Spread your legs for me. I'll point the examination light on you so I can get a good view"

He illuminates his view of the black and pink flesh, the heavy mounted examination light angled on her, warming her and giving him full exposition.. She is unable to see him with the bright light shining in her eyes. He has now unzipped his zipper and exposed himself

"It's here doctor" Beyonce says pointing.

Yvan stopped as Fi in amazement said "That's a good story Yvan"

"Help me out here Fi. What could she have?"

"A Bartholeins abscess Yvan. That's what she's got"

Yvan continued "Zulichoswki moves the light to above Beyonce so she cannot see what he is doing. He inserts three fingers of his right hand and moves it out and in, inside her, playing with himself with his left hand till he shoots out on the examination couch and floor."

Beyonce gets the acrid smell of ejaculate and realises what has happened. She sits up with alacrity and sees his now semi-erect member which he is hastily trying to replace in his trousers.

Angrily she says "What is the meaning of this?"

Dr Stanislaw sheepishly says "Well, I just kind of started liking it and got carried away"

Beyonce is looking aghast.

 He adds "Well, you know I am just a man, not only a doctor."

She hurriedly dresses and walks out of the room saying to the receptionist as she leaves. "Tell that old pervert that my lawyers will be in touch. I'll make sure he never gets close to another patient again."

Fi in admiration says "You learn pretty fast Yvan. I couldn't have told that story better myself. Not antithetical at all to my own version."

"Forced intimate proximity creates problems for sexually charged doctors Fi." He nods sagely "We need to follow-up all these doctors Fi. What happened to Stanislav?"

 "He has returned to his native Poland. Probably working as a doctor there like many other who roam free."

"The newspapers should follow up on all these doctors Fi"

"One of them did but they didn't give a blanket review of all the cases when they did so. They were more interested in which sexually perverted doctor was still practicing. I'll tell you later. Let's go for a walk in Soho and see what's on offer for the single sex obsessed person "

"It's a deal Fi but I want to buy some stuff too. On that guarantee only do I come with you" Fi hadn't realised it but she was holding her breath at his statement. She exhaled slowly

"I suggested it to get rid of the endless grey skies we see; a bit of light entertainment. What sort of stuff do you want to buy?"

"Not sure what we will see."

"Nothing too perverted please Yvan. I may permit you a rubber doll"

"I don't need that Fi I've got my real live doll; you"

19.   **TOY SEX**

The streets of Soho were empty. Corona virus and London's weather had put even the sex crazed off shopping. Most of the shops were shut with Aluminium shutters to prevent robbery but two that sold food and drink were open.

"Smart ploy that. Selling food and drink with sex objects.

Yvan was dreamlike. "I was a boy when I came here. Not nearly a man."

There were videos of all aspects to buy. "Hmm flagellation, lesbianism, threesomes and lady boys. Which do you want Fi?"

"Get what you want Yvan, we can watch it together but make sure you hide it well from Maria"

"Oh look maybe we can try this on our honeymoon?" He was holding up a plastic wrapped   large walnut -sized pink ring.

"That looks a bit small if I think it is what I think it is. Do they come in different sizes?"

"I don't like pink. Do they have blue?"

Yvan found a blue one which was slightly larger.

"What do they do?"

Yvan read the advertising description. 'Makes you last longer; stay harder for longer.

"Wow."

"Look at this rubber job with a secure flange and two solid olive sized lumps." Fi walked over from where she had been looking at the vibrators.

"It's for additional rear stimulation when you have sex Yvan. It's for you. Want to get that?"

"I'll try anything once Fi. It isn't too expensive. Did you want anything?"

"No. Remind me to tell you about that idiotic Asian doctor who wanted to explore sex toys with an unwilling patient."

Walking home from the tube Fi started her story

"He was a gynaecologist who told a patient to bring sex toys to his surgery and wanted to give her porn. Obviously he has been struck off."

Dr Iftekhar Ahmed, 51, even asked the woman if she wanted sex after performing an intimate examination on her.

The married dad-of-two also stared at the patient as she undressed at his surgery in Huddersfield, West Yorkshire - warning her not to tell anyone because he would 'be in trouble'.

Ahmed was found guilty of a string of sexual misconduct offences, including touching the woman intimately without consent and asking if she felt like having sex while examining her. The Medical Practitioners Tribunal Service

(MPTS) heard how the woman, in her 40s, went to the Princess Royal health clinic for advice about sexual health twice in August 2013 and January 2015.

She told how she had been left shaken and embarrassed when Ahmed quizzed her over her sex life, what sex toys she used and if he could look at them.

The woman said: 'He started behaving strangely when I told him I didn't have a boyfriend and he started asking about my sex life and if I was having sex with anyone.

'I said I am having sex with someone because I didn't want him to know I was on my own because I felt uncomfortable and worried.

'He went on to ask many sexual questions like what sexual positions do I do and which I like.'

The woman continued: 'He asked if I like licking and he pulled his tongue out and wiggled it. 'She said: 'I did not answer but I felt dirty.

'He asked me the same question again and I told him again I didn't understand. He then said again did I feel like I wanted to have sex whilst he was doing the exam. I did not answer.'

'I said I wasn't at home and I could feel he was shocked. He paused and he said it was alright, he could come this evening.

'I said I didn't feel that it was alright for him to come round to install porn and I didn't want that.' The woman told how she saw Ahmed 'staring at me when I was putting my clothes back on'.

He would later access her medical records for her telephone number and ask her more inappropriate questions about her private life. He also asked if he could install pornography on her home computer.

The patient said in her statement: 'He said it was Dr Ahmed, did I remember what we said earlier and was it okay for him to come to my house to put the porn on my laptop.

Ahmed, originally from Bangladesh, failed to attend the medical tribunal disciplinary hearing and is now thought to be practising in America. He was banned from the medical register for life.

"You are right there must be a streak of insanity otherwise what makes them think this behaviour is permissible?"

"He was 51. Do men get a sexual madness as they get older Yvan like male menopause? I must look it up. Otherwise why would anyone with any brains do what that idiotic goon did?"

"Do you have a more nuanced understanding of what the patients are going through," Yvan said. "In his case was it unfulfilled passion. His wife probably didn't do anything but the missionary position. No sex toys, not the sweet-tasting poison of whipping" He reared back laughing "Did you see all the flagellation and bondage equipment in there?"

"Usually for the gays I think. Remember that young gay doctor? And there was another guy from Ancona, Italy whose wife probably only did straight sex. He set himself up with his own young sex provider under false pretences.

20.   SADOMASOCHISTIC SEX

A doctor who allegedly regularly sexually and psychologically abused a young girl he brought over from Africa has been indicted on charges of sado-masochistic behaviour, juidicial sources said Wednesday.

The tale began as one of romance and love. An African student in search of new beginnings was brought to Italy by a doctor from Ancona, not immeditaley identified, who enrolled the young hopeful at the University of Perugia, providing her also with a residence permit.

However, the story soon turned sour. The victim described in a statement that, in return for his 'generosity', the doctor would repeatedly force her to meet with him in an apartment, naked, where he would tie her down, push a ball into her mouth and turn up the television volume to quash her screams, and then brutally sexually abuse her. She would allegedly be left with various bruises indicating blows and whip slashes to the neck.

The girl claimed that the nightmare would continue on regular occasions until 2014 when she decided to press charges against her captor. The indictment was accepted Wednesday by prosecutor Cristina Polenzani.

"But no one who did it to a patient?"

"Not in the UK that I could find. There were some other Italian doctors who were indulging in private activities but I'll tell you about that in a moment. No sadism in UK doctors that I can find but one sick Dutch guy working in Liverpool"

"There seem to be lots of weird medics in the Liverpool area." Wasn't that the place that they kept the children's hearts that you mentioned in your book 'Murder in Medicine'?

 Fi nodding said "That's correct but this behaviour is, I think, the background of the man not where he worked. He was a surgeon who sent an online dominatrix explicit photos of himself at work in the Liverpool NHS hospital. He was suspended from his job immediately on being discovered.

"I saw the pictures. Blinds the imagination; that reality going on in a busy surgical theatre."

Dr Leendert Verstraten was a married father-of-two and 55 years old at the time that he took those pictures of himself half-naked in his operating scrubs with sadomasochistic messages scrawled on his stomach. He sent them to Linda Jones, a 40 year old, who he says he paid more than £2,000 to fuel his sexual fantasies.

"How does one meet up with these fetish people?"

"He contacted her via a fetish dating website the year before this incident.

"That seems like easy money. Beating someone and getting paid for it."

"It is degrading Yvan, to the abuser and the abused although a streetwise woman will see that is easier money than having straight sex with the masochist."

Carefully folding up the Sunday Times that he was reading he said "I am all yours" He smiled, took the folded paper and started hitting himself with it chanting " I need beating, I need beating".

Fi laughing said "Stop it or you will make me lose the plot. In one email from Leender he included three different pictures of his genitals padlocked inside a plastic chastity belt designed for 'torture', he said: 'At work operating today. Hope my scrubs don't fall down!'

Ycan said " Ah I focused on the wrong part." He started hitting his genitals.

"You won't get the story Yvan if you continue like that." Fi interjected as he tried to continue his' I need beating' chant. She took his hands in hers.

"In other images, Dr Verstraten's shirt is lifted to reveal messages scrawled on his body in black marker pen. One read 'Owned by Mistress LJ' – the name used by his dominatris.

"Which type of women do this job Fi?"

"Women who need money find this is the easiest way to make it. Mrs Jones was a married mother-of-one, from Blackburn, who never met the doctor in person. In another email he wrote: 'This useless b**** of a slave is owned by Mistress L.'

Other photographs included one of him dressed in stockings and a thong, with his hospital pass around his neck.

"Guess what this pervert earned?"

Yvan now that his hands were out of Fi's grasp fiddled unnecessarily with his copy of the Times and said "100k?"

"Yes. Leender earned around £100,000 a year as an orthopaedic surgeon in Liverpool and the Isle of Man. He sent Linda dozens of sexual images and videos and persuaded her to send him the chastity belt he used in pictures of himself at work including one he sent in an email saying: 'Lock a bit obvious in theatre?'

"How did he take these pictures in the operating theatres?"

"At night? I;m not sure. Bosses at Aintree University Hospital, Liverpool, and Noble's Hospital on the Isle of Man suspended him while they investigated. That may be one of the questions they are asking."

"I'm fascinated by Mrs Jones. Did the Beatles write their song about her" Yvan sang

"Me and Mrs. Jones, We've got a thing going on. We both know it's wrong…"

"Not sure that was the Beatles but I know which song you mean and this event occurred well after the song became a hit."

"Mrs Jones told the Daily Mail she worked as an online dominatrix to 'pay the bills', but was horrified when she realised Dr Verstraten was so obsessed that he was indulging his sexual fantasies at work.

"Hang on Fi I'm looking up the Daily Mail article to see what Mrs. Jones said"

'When I found out he was a surgeon I was horrified,' she said. 'I told him it was wrong and unethical. I told him if anyone found out, he would be ruined.

'If he is in a chastity belt and it gets him going when he is in theatre, it has got to take your mind off the operation. He shouldn't be operating with it on.

'When I knew what he was doing in the hospital, I had enough and knew it had to stop. It made me sick. I've seen and heard a lot of disgusting things, but that was just too far.'

She added: 'Sometimes he messaged to say he'd been in surgery six hours and not stopped thinking of me the entire time.

'It's not right he's allowed to be in a life-or-death situation while daydreaming about some of the most twisted sexual fantasies."

Yvan stood up and said, turning away and walking to the door

"A dominatrix with morals. She needs to change her job. You need people in those positions who will break every rule in the book not report to higher authority" His words floated towards Fi from his turned back "I need a toilet stop" He walked off singing "Me and Mrs Jones"

When he returned he said "My blood curdles and my skin prickles with the goofs these doctors get up to. Why don't they just do it at home?"

"The Italian doctors did but they still got into trouble and if I told the police about the images sent to me by one of the bridge players I met on BBO they would be investigating him as well. He was from Belgium."

"Is that part of Europe full of sicko's?" Yvan's expression was inscrutable.

"You meet up with the strangest people Fi. All sick men. Mentally sick."

"Yes they are in all circles. Harvey Weinstein, Epstein and in on line bridge clubs. The BBO guy was obsessed with having sex in full view of people so he said he wanted to do it on a hotel balcony and the images he sent me were of a woman chained up in leather gear"

"Don't you hate these guys?"

"They are harmless and I did suggest he come to the UK so I could see him in the flesh."

"What? Why did you do that?"

"Curiosity. He wanted me to meet him at the airport in my car so that he could have sex in the car."

"Did you tell him we were together?"

"I am not sure he would have cared. He was married or so he said. Just interested in getting what his wife wasn't providing."

"Why do you give these people your email Fi?"

"Trying to sell my books but if they send me a link I never click on it. He sent me plenty in the bridge game while we were playing together. I said I'd open it later but I never did. So one day he mails me a fetish picture to my email. A girl tied up with leather and chains."

"Were the Italian sadomasochistic doctor couple bridge players? How were they discovered?"

 "Not bridge players. They were two medics in Pisa. They were using surgical equipment to practice sadomasochism."

"In hospital?"

"No; at home but they had the images of their sexual antics on a USB stick. The USB stick was found in a jacket at the local laundrette. It was given to police."

The 47-year-old doctor and his radiologist female partner, 40, were put under investigation after the images of the couple using medical equipment while having sex and other photos of female genitalia were found. This was reported in the Italian newspaper 'Corriere della Sera'

The USB was passed to police in Ponsacco, in the province of Pisa, who went through the couple's laptops, USB sticks, photos and objects to practice sadomasochism.

"They should be struck off" Yvan said.

"The investigation hinges on whether the surgical equipment used belongs to the hospital where the couple works or whether the items were bought by the medics."

The pair argued that the images are private and should not concern authorities.

"Do patients want people like this looking after them?"

"No they don't because it is what is in your mind when you deal with these people that matters. Are they able to dissociate their reality from the fantasy? Gay husband certainly do that. They have a sexual encounter with a man in a park. Ride their bikes home, wash their hands at the sink and then switch in to normal mode saying "I'm preparing salmon for dinner. Who wants some?"

"I wouldn't want to be sharing pizza or pasta with them" Yvan said "Who know what they've used the knives and forks for?"

"I've met guys who wanted to be beaten. The guy I am thinking of was fascinated by being beaten with slippers and asked me whether I had a whip. Sad really. He had bought his wife a most expensive sports car and allowed her to spend his big pension pot as an apology for his thoughts and behaviours."

"What behaviours?"

"When she was away in Spain he would invite me over to the house and suggested I bring my beating equipment with me." Yvan was shaking his head in disbelief

"Did you go?"

"I remember a friend who thought her husband was gay. She questioned me about it a lot of the time and I reassured her that he was not but one day he invited me to a play being held at Richmond theatre. It was about a dominatrix and a guy who wanted to dress in drag. "Josie and the Elvis. He kept trying to assess her behaviour and reaction to the play throughout it. He also took her to see "La cage aux folle" which is about a gay couple and the story of the bisexual author Colin. " Shadowland. It dealt with his lifestyle as a gay man and his later years married to an American lady who he truly loved but in a more spiritual sense."

"Gay husbands. Is that your speciality?"

"Yes he had tried to tell her about his sexuality throughout their life together. It was sad as if she had a mature attitude to it they may have been together to this day and have saved their children a lot of trauma when they were going through their formative years."

"It was a difficult time for her as when he tried to come out the children turned on him saying "Daddy's been lying to us all these years."

"They refused to accept his sexuality?"

"Yes so he had to go back to pretending he wasn't gay although he had been a practising homosexual all his life.

"Even when she married him?"

"Apparently he gave up for a period of time but then started again when a young attractive gay man joined his workplace and seduced him back along the gay path."

"That song I've written on "you tube –Is he gay- and whose song lyrics appear in my poetry book 'Naughty poems for naughty people' is about this guy and his behaviours."

 It was very sad as he was so addicted to gay sex that he couldn't stop soliciting in parks toilets and public places. " Alleyways in Twickenham where gay men went, toilets below the Richmond Waitrose shopping mall, The Tesco rooftop car park on Cromwell Road, Richmond Park and Ham Common. The toilets at Kingston gate He knew them all as potential hunting grounds and before they divorced he tried to show her all his hunting grounds."

"That was odd behaviour?"

"Yes it was odd but I believe he was trying his best to make her understand what he was doing and to get her to accept him."

"I dedicated the song on you tube to Phillip Schofield as he came out as being a gay man after 15 years of marriage. He had two beautiful daughters."

"I've forgotten. Who is Phillip Schofield?"

"He is the breakfast television presenter. He announced his gayness on TV although he had probably warned his wife that the announcement was coming. I thought it was very courageous."

"You don't let me watch much TV Fi that's why I don't know him"

"It is a mindless activity Yvan and it is a very good way of 'socially distancing' people.

"Although when I start writing my next book you will be a ' book widower' as I will be stuck to my computer typing 8 hours a day and you will have to amuse yourself however you wish. TV, Maria, pornography or BBO- Bridge on line.

"Are you jealous of Maria?"

"No. She is wonderful. You are lucky to have her."

"Going back to your friend and her gay ex-husband. Was he into masochism?"

"He had told her this story of a school master in his school who wore a gas mask and gave the boys canings when they did wrong. Making them pull down their trousers and exposing their bare bottoms which he caned."

"Sounds like a sick bastard school teacher to me. Was that in the sixties?"

"Yes. The odds were not good that these male children would end up sexually normal but she thinks he was exploring his sexuality at the time of divorce and that he never exposed his true sexuality with her.".

"Why did she think that?"

"He was reading Alexandra McCall Smith's book "How to walk in high heels" and she found a long red glove in the house and a large black cloth which he couldn't explain away."

"Was he into snuff activities?"

"Oh no no. She thinks he used to use it to dress in drag. It was his Audrey Hepburn look.

"That and the glove?"

"Not only that. He would use his children's panties. She would see him in the night rifling through the dirty-linen basket at the top of the stairs and she thought that was what he was doing"

"Why didn't he use clean ones?"

"I think everyone would see they had been stretched to man size whereas the dirty ones would go in the wash and shrink back to original size after washing."

"He was fog blinded" Yvan said "No clear vision of how to proceed"

"He watched breakfast at Tiffany's and I think he pretended to be Audrey Hepburn."

"Why didn't he just admit to it all? Drag? Bisexuality? His feelings?"

"I have no idea. It takes courage like Phillip Schofield."

Yvan said "I think someone was going to out Schofield that's why he came out of the closet"

"You mean like Mark Oaten the liberal democrat who was tipped to be the Leader of the Liberal Democrats until he was outed by a gay prostitute?"

"Uhuh. Mark Oaten was married and had two children. The gay prostitute reported him to the newspapers and his political career ended.

"Feef let's go to bed. " I want to have simple straight sex with you. No prostitutes. Nothing too strenuous."

The yearning to kiss Fi swelled in Yvans mind but she was blissfully ignorant continuing her story

"Her husband did say to his wife that he could have told his Mum but he could never tell his dad."

"Was that why he never came out?"

"I think so. That; the attitude of his children; attitude to that generation of men being gay, all of those factors. Now his dad is dead and his mother has gone as well so he should be able to speak the truth but he doesn't. His children don't care if he is or he isn't so I am not sure why he doesn't just come out and tell the truth."

"It's several years on Fi isn't it? He should try coming out now. It's so much easier."

"I don't think he would want his wife's accusations at the time to be proved correct so he will go to his grave pretending to be heterosexual when he is actually bi."

"And he is currently cheating the young lady he chose to replace his wife, the first 'beard'

"Yes I've heard that expression. 'Beard' Gay men of that era married to hide the fact that they were homosexuals. Their wives were the beards"

"Your friend has a story that needs to be written Fi but I need to hold you close and sink my longings into your being. It's platonic sex tonight."

"I think that's called love Yvan"

He rose from the couch singing "I wanna hold your hand. I wanna hold your hand."

Fi joined in and they sang the Beatles song together mounting the spiral staircase, Yvan holding on to the circular 18th century iron railing and wooden rail post. He leaned on her as they mounted and she did not leave his side slowing her steps to match his pace.

"Why did you never have children of your own Yvan?"

"Never wanted them Fi. I've got yours now so I don't need any. I live their stories through your eyes and that is more than enough for me.

"You should write your friend's story of her being married to a gay husband Fi"

"Phillip Schofield has already written his book Yvan so I am not sure whether mine would sell as well."

"We've deviated a bit Fi. You were telling me about masochism and your other friend and we've gone to gay husbands"

"They are all mysteriously linked through I think the British public school system. The way they sexually and physically abused boys and made them fear men, may be linked closely to gay sexual experiences.

"I need to investigate it more."

"Actually you are wrong Fi."

"Why do you say that?"

"I found an Osteopath in Florida who was in to that sort of deviancy. He didn't use the British schoolboy system."

"Oh ok. Which one?"

"Here have a read in the Florida Health News"

A Lake Worth family doctor accused of sadistic "punishment therapy" that involved handcuffs, blindfolds, whips and other implements of torture apologized repeatedly to the Board of Osteopathic Medicine. That was not enough to persuade board members that Dr. David Simon could safely continue to practice.

The board voted to "counter-offer" with revocation -- the only action it could take in this type of hearing. The vote amounts to marching orders to the state DOH: Don't settle the case, go after his license.

Only one board member voted against the motion to seek revocation. Dr. Anna Hayden said the board usually allows doctors who have committed sexual misconduct to continue practicing on probation, with a monitor. She said she thought the board should be "consistent."

"You see what I mean Yvan. They allow sexually weird health care preofessionals to continue to practice, not realising that by doing so they are giving them license to continue to perpetrate these acts."

But other board members rejected the notion that this was an ordinary case.

"If there was ever a time that this board would revoke a license for sexual misconduct, this is it," said Dr. Ronald Burns, board chairman. "We cannot have an osteopathic physician behaving like this."

"You'll find out this is a fantasy," his attorney predicted. "She's spinning all these tales."

While that doesn't make it okay that Simon had an affair with a patient, the attorney said, "It wasn't torture. It was adventurous sex between two adults." He said Dr. Simon was prominent in the community, where he has practiced for 28 years. He had no prior discipline on his license.

Simon denied that he tortured the patient, identified only by her initials, CK. But he conceded that what he did was "inappropriate," that it "crossed a boundary."

The case ruined his reputation and career, he said. "I can't excuse it. ... I'm embarrassed for myself, and it has devastated my wife."

The Palm Beach County Sheriff's Office began investigating after CK and her mental-health counsellor called to report the abuse. CK told a detective that Simon suggested the after-hours sessions at his office, which she called "punishment therapy," as a treatment for her severe depression. She said she didn't like it but submitted to it because he told her it had helped others.

The detective then went to Simon's office, where he obtained the doctor's consent for a search. In an exam room, the detective said, he found whips, chains, blindfolds, handcuffs and sexual paraphernalia.

Simon told the detective that he and CK had a consensual sexual relationship that began after she was no longer his patient.

Investigators found he had prescribed medicine for CK several times during the year that the sadomasochistic sessions continued. In any event, Florida law bars doctors from turning their patients into sex partners, whether it is consensual or not, because it is considered an abuse of power.

"That is true, worldwide Yvan certainly in the UK."

CK told investigators she wanted to stop the sessions but was afraid Simon would hurt her if she did. She also needed the medication samples he gave her, she said.

But after a scary three-hour torture session in November 2011, she said, she decided she could not continue. She said Simon left her tied up in a closet for quite a while; after letting her out, she said, he choked her and whipped her repeatedly.

The following month she attempted suicide and was hospitalized, the records show. After her release she asked her counsellor to help her file a complaint.

Because Simon had been CK's family doctor for years, he knew of her fragile mental state, members of the board said. "She was damaged, and you manipulated her," Burns said. "You subjected her to mental and physical torture." Simon responded, "Was it torture? Not really. It was inappropriate behavior. I'm not sure I'd consider it torture. ...At no point in time did I coerce her, threaten her."

Burns came back with this: "Do you think anyone would consent to being choked?" Simon said quietly, "No."

In pressing for revocation, Dr. Joel Rose called the case "the most egregious one I've seen." He said Simon showed "predatory behavior."

"What amazes me is how they think they can get away with their behaviour and not be found out"

21. **CHILLING SEX**

It was the next evening. Fi had worked on her book all day and Yvan had done some trading and Forex. The weather hadn't improved. The wind was whipping round the trees; rain spattering on the glass pane trickling in rivulets making geometric patterns around dust motes. Yvan had dosed off in his chair after dinner. He awoke disoriented. "Fi" he shouted.

There was no answer. He felt a panic attack. 'One day I will wake and she won't be here' he thought.

"Fi" he shouted again, anxiety mounting.

Pain hovered in his mind and a sick feeling in his stomach as he mounted the stairs. Then he heard the bathroom door open. Relief flooded over him.

She was warm and fresh smelling after her bath. In her oversize T shirt with wet hair she still looked unbelievably beautiful. "I miss you when you are not around" he said

"I saw you had fallen asleep. I didn't want to disturb you."

"One day you will go Fi."

"Yvan I'm here forever. I will always love you."

"Even after I die?"

"I told you Yvan. I will fight for your life even if you are a hundred years old. Fight the ghastly killing doctors who bump off oldies."

"But will you love me after I die? Will you love me forever."

"Well I won't love you like Tanzler loved Elena that's for sure."

"Tanzler?"

"Get ready for bed Yvan and I'll tell you Tanzler's story" She cocked her head in the direction of the bathroom door. "I'll get into bed and wait for you."

"I fancy a soak today Fi. Not a shower. You could put your feet in my bath to stay warm."

"Tanzler's story isn't that kind of story Yvan you will not get a boner. It is sad and slightly sick."

"Was he a doctor?"

"Worked in Xray in Key West, Florida; the hunting ground of my Scientologist ex- boyfriend"

Yvan turned on the shower welcoming the hot fountain gushing on his cold skin. He had cooled down while he was dozing and the fire in his front room had burnt down to embers. He rushed his shower, ill-prepared to return to bed and find Fi asleep.

Towelling himself he thought 'How can she love me?' Catching sight of his paralysed left arm and leg"

"Tanzler, Fi" he said when finally he crawled under the bed covers and ran his fingers through her now nearly drying hair.

Fi put down her copy of 'Obama' that she was reading and downed the last of her camomile and ginger tea turning obligingly towards him.

"I want you very close for all kinds of reasons Fi but they aren't sexual. I just love you."

They kissed softly. Yvan overcome by his emotions giving an uncertain smile when they stopped.

"I'm afraid Tanzler is the most famous story of what modern day medicine calls 'Necrophilia'- sex with the dead. His is the most famous case although one of the newspapers a few years ago did an article about a mortuary technician who cut off the erect member of a handsome young man before they buried him. Not sure what she used it for especially since it had embalming fluid in it."

"Wouldn't that numb your parts?"

"I have no idea. Anyway back to 1930, and Carl Tanzler who was living in Key West, Florida when he met Elena Hoyos.

Elena had checked in to the United States Marine Hospital where Tanzler was working as an X-ray technician. She had tuberculosis (TB). TB was a death sentence in the thirties. Elena was a 21-year-old Cuban woman whose husband had left her, though they were still legally married as she had not divorced. Tanzler was 55 at the time Elena was admitted.

He was a German, who had left his family in another part of Florida to live alone in Key West.

"That is strange behaviour."

"Even more strange, he greatly exaggerated his accomplishments and called himself Count von Cosel though he wasn't a count."

"I guess he thought that pretending power and privilege would give him an edge in the love stakes?"

Tanzler was obsessed with Elena. He tried desperately to cure her disease. He ignored the hospital's protocol and the boundaries of his own job description, playing doctor with at-home treatments and homemade medicines which he administered to her.

He smothered her with love offerings and marriage proposals.

"Did she love him in return?"

"It's doubtful she reciprocated his feelings. She had TB which used to be known as 'Consumption'. She was just trying to survive the disease ravaging her body. Tanzler's unauthorized cures didn't work, and Elena died in 1931 a year later. Tanzler personally bought a mausoleum to house her remains. Unbeknownst to her family, he was the only one with the key and would visit the mausoleum late at night to be with her. He also had a telephone installed in the mausoleum so they could talk regularly.

"And all this time he was carrying out his job in the Xray Department? Re3meber my stories about psychotic nurses in the book 'Murder in Medicine'? No one who knows these people suspect they have aberrant thinking"

"Yes. There are lot's of odd people that one works with and the staff put up with them because the Hospital doesn't fire them. I've known many in my time."

Yvan said "I'm getting hot" unbuttoning the silk pyjama top and removing it,

"Tanzler did the opposite to Elena Yvan. Two years after Elena's death, Tanzler secretly removed her body and towed it to his home in a child's wagon. He later claimed that through one of their conversations, Elena had instructed him to do so.

Tanzler filled Elena's corpse with rags, secured her bones with wire, and mended her skin with wax and plaster.

"Wasnt her body rotting?"

"It was but he was determined to do his best with what was left. He dressed the body in Elena's own clothes and a wig of her own hair. He inserted a glass eyes and disguised the smell of decay with perfume.

"Did he have sex with her or just companionship?"

"He made a makeshift vagina from a paper tube so he could have sex with the corpse."

"Fi he is insane"

"I am afraid so." Yvan placed himself at eye level with Fi's breasts as he adjusted his position in bed. He nuzzled her.

"Tanzler also had an airship which he created which he bizarrely intended to use to launch Elena's corpse into space, which he thought would resurrect her and turn back the clock on her body's decay. In 1940, suspicious that something weird was going on, Elena's sister Florinda went to Tanzler's house. She found the disturbing scene and contacted the police."

"Did they jail him for life?"

"Tanzler was arrested for grave robbing, but he ended up walking free because the statute of limitations on the crime had already passed as it was 10 years later."

The body was removed from Tanzlers home and placed on view for the public at a local funeral home. It was a giant spectacle, attracting over 6,000 people, including the press. Many chose to romanticize the story, seeing Tanzler as a man entwined in a tragic love tale.

"He was obsessed FI"

"I am not sure what you call it Yvan. He may well have been. For the rest of his life, Carl Tanzler longed for Elena. He didn't seem to know where the bounds of reality were. He asked for her corpse to be given back to him, but it was buried in an unmarked grave by this time so he was never able to find it.

"I do not know whether to feel sad for him or revolted Fi"

"Don't be quick to judge him Yvan or to take the moral high ground as most people did. No one has a clue to what was going on in his brain. The pictures on the internet don't say much."

"There are pictures on the internet?"

"Yes; of him and of the original Elena and the waxwork dummy Elena."

"Ok Fi I'll give him the benefit of the doubt and feel sorry for him"

"There is another twist to this tale Yvan and I do think it may have been obsessional love because when he died in 1952, he was found with another horrifying creation...a life-size doll wearing a plaster death mask of Elena and recreated to look like her."

Yvan's eyes showed contempt. "He does not get my sympathy. He is mentally sick and a pervert."

"I think everyone felt that because I couldn't find pictures of the last doll like Elena on the internet ; just a drawing.

"Why did he keep this prolonged and exquisite torture going Fi?"

"He had no replacement to help him forget her. It is what I have always believed. When you leave somebody you should find someone else otherwise you will be stuck with your unfulfilled longings."

"Is that why you are with me Fi? To forget the Scientologist?" There was a tremble in his voice.

"No; not at all. He and I are still in touch. I managed to put our relationship on a different footing. He is not as handsome as you are Yvan; quite ugly really. It was his music that attracted me but now I'm in love with another musician's work. Loudon Wainwright III whose voice and compositions I am enamoured of"

Long seconds ticked by as Yvan digested this information. "You still communicate with him?" Fi could see his mental gyrations.

"Relax Yvan I've told him to go back to his wife as any good Scientologist would"

"I want to see your email communications Fi." His voice faltered."I did not know you were still in touch."

"Of course you can see them but you do not need to worry. He treated me badly before we broke up and I believe the Maya Angelou line."

"Which one?"

"If someone treats you badly once don't give them the opportunity to treat you badly again"

"I will never go back to him"

"You should be more worried about that gorgeous young 21 year old bridge player who is targeting me?"

"Who?"

"Jay"

"He is so junior Fi although he is a great player."

"He is a member of the English junior team"

"Forget about Jay. He is not a threat. Go to sleep now. In the morning after breakfast let us sit on the sofa and I can tell you about having sexual feelings for juniors and the quote of another ex boyfriend of mine a Cardiologist who said 'Never f-ck the junior staff'"

"Why did he say that?"

"If you do you cannot keep control of them. And there is the danger of losing your job when things go sour."

22.　　**JUNIOR SEX**

"Some of the junior doctors that I have worked with look like iconic glamour models."

"I bet you were pretty stunning"

"Yes I must have been. I was the block queen"

"What is that?"

"Equivalent to a Prom Queen. I was queen of the Anatomy block."

"Queen of the dead bodies? That is not very flattering"

"Queen of the first year of Medical School." Fi was thinking back to her time as a Medical Student

"Juniors are prey for the Senior Consultants. I was preyed upon by a doctor who has now become a born again Christian. He was a surgeon and I went to him because I had a cyst under my right arm and he tried to kiss me. I think he was married at the time."

"Yes I've seen the scar under your right arm. The skin is stretched so tightly. He couldn't have been a very good surgeon. The scar is so obvious."

"Probably more interested in the sexual aspects of me than the surgery."

"Probably too close to your gorgeous breasts to concentrate on the cyst" Yvan leered at her breasts as he said it laughing mirthfully. Then more seriously

"I've never made a sexual advance without thinking it through Fi. In your case you were open and inviting that was why I kissed you the first time." His features were schooled his mind deep in thought about their first encounter.

"Lot's of seniors get away with doing inappropriate things with juniors because they think they won't be found out or reported because the junior does not know what is appropriate behaviour.

"He should know he can't kiss you"

 "Yes of course but some people just play it for whatever they can get. Dr Palaniappan Saravanan was sacked by the hospital trust for gross misconduct. He was a heart specialist at Arrowe Park Hospital. He was struck-off the medical register after his "disgraceful" sexual harrassment of five junior female doctors.

"They should find it necessary to erase all such doctor's names from the register Fi."

They imposed an immediate order of suspension to cover the 28-day period in which Saravanan would be entitled to appeal and found him wanting.

"I do not know how he thought he would get away with deliberate and sexually motivated touching of five junior female doctors - on the ward in front of patients and other nursing staff."

"Primal urge Fi allows every caution to be thrown to the wind"

They did a 60-page report says that on all possible occasions he specifically chose young female doctors to accompany him on ward rounds.

The report said: This selectivity suggested an element of deliberate planning on Dr Saravanan's part in order to facilitate opportunities to make physical contact with the doctors.

His inappropriate behaviour started with what might simply have been perceived as over-friendly touching of the back or shoulders but this was escalated to touching the doctors on other parts of their bodies including an intimate area, notably the bottom, and on two occasions he touched bare skin.

"They didn't complain for a very long time. Finally they did"

His actions had a distressing impact on each of the doctors. They felt they could not complain for fear of jeopardising their careers."

"There is touching and there is touching Fi. I liked the way you touched people when you talked to them"

"Never on a bottom Yvan; just on an arm. Corona has got rid of any touching now; nor can I even smile warmly at anyone."

"I think people do know you are warm and welcoming Fi even with a mask. Your voice is friendly and joyous."

"What else did the report say?"

One junior known in the report as "Dr E" gave a very graphic description of events and used such terms as "sick, terrified and trapped" to describe how the ordeal had made her feel.

Part of Dr E's statement said: "He was standing so close that the front of his body was touching my back and I felt trapped.

"I let go and tried to move away but he initially didn't move. He then let me get out of his grasp.

Another junior known as "Dr A" carried out a scan on a patient under supervision of Saravanan: "For the duration of the scan Dr Saravanan kept his hand on my bottom.

"He held the centre of my left buttock cheek with a firm grip, every now and then stroking with his index finger.

"This lasted for roughly five minutes for the duration of the scan.

"I had the probe in my right hand and reached around to the left side of the patient to scan their chest.

"Dr Saravanan held the computer monitor in his right hand and put his left hand on my bottom and began stroking it with his fingers. I think it would have been his index and middle finger that he used."

 She said "I was mortified."

Saravanan provided his own witness statement and also gave spoken evidence via video-link. His account was consistent in denying any intentional sexually motivated touching. Saravanan described his background and the circumstances of his upbringing.

He said he had always been "a tactile person." But the tribunal did not accept Saravanan's assertion that he was generally tactile and that was the reason why he would touch his colleagues.

"Of course he was tactile, the pervert. He just wanted to cop a quick feel"

Witnesses only noticed him touching junior female doctors and not male or more senior female colleagues or nurses or ward clerks.

It felt like Dr Saravanan was taking advantage of the fact that I was a junior, as I was an FY1 at the time. It made me want to get the ward round over and done with so that I could leave.

Dr C: He gradually moved round to touch my right thigh over my clothing. When I realised that, I immediately stood up and moved away.

Dr D: Yes, during ward rounds he would touch me on the bottom, using the back of his hand. Later on during the placement he would turn his hand so the flat of his hand would be touching me.

Dr Saravanan would come up by my side and touch my bottom with the back of his hand. He kept it flat the whole time and deadly still on the centre of my bottom. This occurred on every ward round.

Dr E: Whenever we were with patients or if I was writing up patient notes, Dr Saravanan would stand very close to me and put his hand on the side of my bum or on my bum and move it back and forth which made me feel very uncomfortable.

I was by the computer reviewing notes before seeing a patient and he would put his hand on my bum or my leg.

 "Where did he work?"

"Wirral University Teaching Hospital"

"Professor Letch" Yvan said smoothing his hair

"These sexual offenders seem to be all old ugly and ethnic. Don't you have any gorgeous hotties committing sex acts?"

"I've told you about Thiotepa Yvan. She was gorgeous. There was also a very nice looking doctor who crossed the threshold which he did not need to do.

"Who was that? A woman?"

"Man; Julian Proctor. He was probably arrogant and full of his own charm as handsome guys are. He was 37 when he was struck off. There are pictures of him standing by a sports car"

"What could a handsome young man do that would get him struck off? Why didn't he just form a relationship with somebody?"

"I have no idea. He looked handsome enough to have someone, anyone be attracted to him so how he got himself into this mess is anybody's guess."

"Why aren't people in medicine simple and goodhearted like you?"

"I think it is intrinsic to your genes and very little to do with upbringing although that does count."

He sent a junior medic 900 explicit messages in nine days in a 'relentless' sexual harassment campaign

Julian Proctor, 37, reportedly told a disciplinary panel that the woman 'wanted a piece of the pie'

"See what I mean Yvan? He thought so much of himself he thought all women should fall at his feet."

Julian Proctor, 37, slapped the junior medic's bottom and also sent her pictures and videos of himself showering and performing a sex act.

"Another guy who likes to show his tackle to unwilling women."

The junior doctor, who is in her 20s, repeatedly told him she had a boyfriend so he just didn't think she could refuse, to quote him ' a piece of the pie'

"Proctor was "relentless" in his pursuit for sex wasn't he?"

"Mad. On one occasion he tried to hug her in a lift before slapping her bottom when she tried to avoid his advances.

He had bent over her and asked: "How much do you fancy me?'

"That egotistical behaviour was not made for medicine Fi. He is also narcissistic and at age 37 does not know what is right and what is wrong "

"She reported him but to send 900 texts and many pictures with no encouragement is lunacy personified"

"I hope he is licking his wounds in repentant mode Fi now that he has no job and no income."

"He should have been like 'hairline'. He would never have got into this trouble"

"Hairline?"

"Yes. That was his nickname at the Manchester Royal Infirmary (MRI). He was a nice looking guy but had crooked bottom teeth so didn't smile very often.

"Tell me his story like a story Fi. I feel the need for some sensual activity and a warm cosy bed. Let's go in the bath together and the soapy water will help relax and enhance my nocturnal activities"

"So long as I can jump out of the bath before your nocturnal emissions Yvan"

23. HAIRLINE SEX

"Hairline was a junior doctor at the MRI. He never took control of any situation allowing things to flow naturally towards its conclusion. He did this with his work and with his life. He was a vacillator. His mother could have sworn and threatened but this did not work. He was not biddable."

"There appeared to be no ostensible purpose to his life. He followed the philosophy of 'I just had to do it'. He did not think about his career pathway preferring to let life take him where it wanted"

"I've met men like that; the drifters. Some of them do find their feet."

"Yes; eventually hairline did but he spent his time at the MRI in blissful abandonment to the pleasures of the flesh."

"What did he do?"

"He… "

"No no describe an episode as it happened Fi from your imagination"

The strawberry blonde nurse on Ward 56 has heard a rumour about hairline. She accosts him as he comes on the ward. "Doctor can you look at Mrs. Guthrie She has got a temperature."

"Sure" he says in his Northern Accent looking down at her nurses uniform pushed outwards by her size 38 breasts.

He examines Mrs. Guthrie, prescribes antibiotics and asks strawberry blonde to take blood tests which he writes up. They chat and she touches his hand as he passes her the blood test pathology forms. Hairlines groins are stirring. Strawberry notices this occurring under his pale cream chino's. The rumour spread about him is true. Anything makes him excited. His tackle is always a hairline breadth away from being ready

"Doctor I've got a spare ticket for a concert with Neil Diamond tomorrow. Would you like to come?" She walks over to the blood trolley as she talks making sure he can see her whole body and the curves of her buttock

"I'm off duty tomorrow so could I drop it off with you tonight? I have to go home to get it" She flashes her breasts under the uniform noticing the bulge in the chino's getting bigger.

"When are you going off duty? I can bring it to your room"

"He wanted what she was offering Fi. He could have said leave it on the ward or at reception I guess"

"She wanted what he was offering. What he offered to everyone who turned up at his door. This was how he got the name 'Hairline' He didn't turn anybody down"

"I'm in Room 28 in the Hospital Accommodation block. Pick up a pizza from Pizzeria Castello. We can share it."

Strawberry rushes home washes and dresses and stops by Pizzeria Castello picking up a 12' Pizza Margherita, the cheapest Pizza on the menu.

When she gets to Flat 28 hairline opens the door when she rings the bell. He is wearing Birkenstock sandals and a blue, short sleeved Ralph Lauren T shirt over tracksuit bottoms.

He doesn't offer her coffee or a drink although the half empty bottle of red wine is on the table in the room. The table is illuminated from the light from the road dispatching the darkness of the room. Hairline does not bother to switch the overhead light on.

There is no need for a slow seduction. He knows why strawberry is here. He takes the pizza from her hand and places it on the table. His hands are in her coat tugging it from her shoulders. As it slides to the ground his mouth is pressing down on hers hungrily. Tongues intertwine. He moves from her mouth to her throat. He is forcing her towards the bed. She is making primitive sounds of need. He pushes her onto the faded cream of the hospital bed cover. She feels the hard surface of the foot of the bed under her back. He dislodges her underwear and goes into her between the thin edge of silk covering her wetness and her opened thighs. He kisses her again each kiss becoming deeper and more intense.

She says as he thrusts in to her. "I want to eat you, to suck you, to lick you." The words seem to propel him and he comes rapidly in short gasps. He lies on top of her his weight pressing on her breasts. She lies there feeling his weight and thinking "That was quick"

He is half dosing but now reawakens. He reaches for her panties and pushes impatiently at them trying to remove them. He can smell the musky aroma of their intertwined secretions. Once the panties are removed he moves to the snap fasteners on her silky purple dress. They tear open and his fingers reveal the luscious rounds half covered by her bra. His fingers brush over the skin and his mouth descends to suck and bite gently then harder. He enters her again mouth pressing over hers. She hooks her legs around his hips as he pushes her bare bottom. His nails dig into her flesh. They were strange nails, flat and crooked but they heightened her pleasure. The discomfort from his body, his nails and the rapid thrusting movements add to her moment of pleasure. He does not wait till she orgasms as he lets himself go with wave after wave of pleasure.

She remains silent feeling sordid and used. Remorse fills her. Yes she had wanted sex but where was the build up? The wining and dining and getting to know each other? Maybe the Neil Diamond concert would help tomorrow

Strawberry realises she hadn't just wanted sex. She had wanted a relationship with him. Could she have a relationship with him? She was a 40 year old, married night sister and he was a 28 year old stag who shafted anyone who turned up at his door.

She surveys him with a baleful eye as he eases himself off her, reaching for a tissue from the bedside table she wipes away her sticky warmth. He bends and pulls up his track suit bottoms which he had not bothered to remove from his legs.

She says nothing. All this time he has said nothing.

"Would you like to take a shower? The communal bathroom is at the end of the hall."

He hands her his towel which is still wet from the shower he has had previously.

Without bothering to show her where the shower is, he opens the pizza box and ravenously starts devouring the pizza. By the time she returns 2/3rds has been devoured. The rest is cold

Her pride is wounded. He offers her the wine. She can see he wants her to leave so he can be on his own. Awkwardly she discusses the arrangements for tomorrow night. "I'll meet you at the box office at 7 pm."

She had wanted him to ask her to stay the night but twice in one night was more than enough for him. His mouth had hardened and become almost cruel. A feeling of anger flashed through her.

"She asked for it" Yvan said. "He had a reputation for providing a service; not for having relationships"

"They did end up having a relationship of sorts. He would have sex with her on the ward at night if he could and as a night sister she would come to his room when she finished her shift. She mothered him and provided sexual comfort. He was nearly the same age as her son

"The cuckholded husband never found out?"

"No not like the story of Hugh Simpson which rocked the Royal Berks."

"Hugh was the diabetic consultant at the Royal Berkshire Hospital. He was having an affair with the diabetic nurse, the diabetic sister who was married"

"Hang on wasn't that the same hospital as the fortune losing voyeur?"

"Yes Jonathon Fielden."

 "So what happened?"

"The husband found out about Hugh's affair came into the diabetic clinic and assaulted Hugh"

"Was it serious?"

"More like wounded pride I think"

"I hope Hugh is still with the nurse but Reading was full of that sort of thing. Tucked out in the sticks they were all indulging in some sexual activity or another. I was not viewed favourably because I didn't participate"

"You didn't give in to desire?"

"No. I was in love with my husband and didn't need anyone else. I was only interested in forging back the frontiers of science but this was where the perv doctor was looking at naked women on the hospital computer and where the Zimbabweaian locum was always trying to get his hand in my knickers."

"No cheese and porn parties though? Like the Canadians?"

"I heard that at some of the social gatherings they had a car key lottery?"

"What?"

"Apparently at the start of the evening you threw your car key into a pot by the front door. At the end of the evening you had to go home with whoever had your car key."

"How did you get out of that one?"

"My car key stayed in my handbag. I didn't want to end up with a man who I would not have wanted to have sex with under normal circumstances. There were some who were young and gorgeous and attractive but they weren't for me as I was married"

"Weren't they all married?"

"They were but morality was low on their agenda of requirements for being a successful consultant."

"It was a bit like the directors casting couch. People thought you had to sleep with the top bosses to succeed. This usually worked. A Consultant Haematologists at a top London institution is only though to have achieved her successes because she was free with her sexual favours to her predecessor who held the position

"And I missed a professorship by refusing to sleep with him."

"The more immoral you are the higher you appear to rise? The fortune losing voyeur was a top dog wasn't he?"

"Yes. The earth was whipped up by these sex crazed doctors and patient care was only and excuse for the hidden sex mad romps."

"You didn't include this as a reason for deaths in your book 'Murder in Medicine.'"

"I'm not sure it was but if someone is shagging the nurse can he concentrate on the patient?"

"Wasn't that what the dominatrix thought of that Dutch bloke... what was his name?" "Leendert Verstraten"... "and why she reported him?"

 "Yes it was. On that basis all these sex crazed idiots should not be allowed to practice by the GMC because their brains are in their bollocks. They are dealing with life and death situations and should only be concentrating on work not on their genitals.

"But they are continuing to work. I wonder why?"

24.   THEY ROAM FREE

"Most people, like me, don't report all the minor sexual infringements that occur. I reported the computer-using nude-picture watcher because of those computer incidents not because he made sexually charged comments to me. It indicates the spectrum of their psyche. He still roams free; and all the other doctors who have grabbed me. They will be continuing to slip their hands under the skirts of other doctors."

"What on earth do you mean?"

"About their hands? Grabbing and fondling?"

"No, no, about roaming free"

The Guardian did an article and so did the Daily Mail

More than 1 in 6 doctors convicted of sex offences are still free to practise medicine, the health regulator has admitted.

Since 2013, some 73 doctors have been subject to fitness to practise proceedings following their conviction but the General Medical Council (GMC) has only erased 60 of them from the medical register, leaving the remaining 13 able to practise.

"And these are people who have been reported. Several are unreported"

The GMC refused to say if it knew whether the 13 convicted sex offenders are still working in medicine and, if so, what area of the NHS they are based.

"Sex offences are often premeditated offences by individuals who tend to repeat patterns of behaviour. Such offences represent a much greater breach of trust than simple errors made in good faith under pressure."

"One should not hesitate to tell them straight away that their behaviour is inappropriate and that on the next occasion they will be reported to higher authority." Fi was nodding wisely.

"But why allow them to continue to practice?"

"The GMC were asked what their explanation was Yvan. They did have a good answer for the newspapers. See what you think."

25.   NEWSPAPER SEX

"What was their explanation?"

"Let me read out this article that Paul Bentley published on 24 September 2012 in THE DAILY MAIL.

Dozens of doctors have kept their jobs despite being convicted of serious sex offences.

Medical chiefs claim they cannot ban all sex offenders from working because it might breach their human rights.

At least 31 male GPs, consultants and surgeons are practising even after having assaulted women, been in possession of child pornography or solicited prostitutes.

"That's Rupert Pemsell and Robert Barnett right? The prosssie seekers"

"Yes."

"I guess you could find out about your doctor by looking up the internet?"

"That's how I know about all these cases Yvan. It's not a bleak landscape of my past experiences unlike "Murder in Medicine" where I spoke a lot of truth about my own personal evidence."

 Paul Bentley said 'None of the patients have been informed about their past activities. Some of those with child pornography offences are even believed to be free to treat children.'

"Let's hope whoever employs them doesn't allow them anywhere near children."

"That would be difficult to do. In a family practice mothers would turn up with their children so these people are near their target victims"

"The GMC allows them. Why? Are they so lacking in doctors?"

"That's a good question. Paul Bentley didn't ask it of the GMC"

"Did he ask the GMC?"

Yes. 'Three of the doctors with child pornography convictions are allowed to practise without any conditions, the GMC admitted after a freedom of information request. Individual hospitals are free, however, to impose their own sanctions on the doctors.'

'The GMC insists it inquired about an automatic ban on doctors who are on the sex offenders register but 'advice was obtained from a leading QC who concluded that an automatic bar, without exceptions, would not be compatible with human rights legislation'.

"What about the rights of patients? Wouldn't people be horrified to learn a sex offending doctor had examined them?"

'Katherine Murphy, of the Patients Association, said: 'The GMC has a duty of care to protect the public. It must take all adequate measures to ensure patient safety always comes first.'

Critics of the system want permanent bans on convicted doctors and are concerned that the GMC, which regulates the medics, has no access to the sex offenders register and relies on the police to inform its officials of court sentences.

"But they get it wrong all the time and this is just one more example of it Fi"

The Daily Mail found that of 31 licensed doctors with convictions for sex offences, four have records of sexual assaults, four have been convicted of child pornography offences, two committed voyeurism or exposure offences and 21 solicited prostitutes or were caught kerb-crawling.

"The last two offences, kerb crawling appear harmless. I'd allow them to work but I certainly would not allow the others to continue working"

'A spokesman added that the decision on whether to strike off a doctor was taken by an independent panel of experts and could not be appealed against by the GMC.

That so called independent panel is the Medical Practitioners tribunal (MPTS). They again have the formulaic approach to the apologetic offender. "

"You are a Christian Fi. Shouldn't you be forgiving them malen'kiy?"

"Forgiving is one aspect Yvan forgetting that they offended and have capacity to offend again is quite a different matter. I love it when you call me little one. Sounds nice in Russian malen'kiy"

'The GMC is also looking to automatically strike off doctors who have been convicted of sexual offences. It doesn't have that power at the moment,' he added.

"There are sexual offences for which they should be struck off but if they are kerb crawling for sex what harm is there in that?"

"It is because a certain standard of behaviour is expected in doctors and that is not one that is on the list Yvan"

"You've certainly showed me that doctors are not the boring people I thought they were."

"You should have known that from associating with me Yvan."

"Sadly Fi you are boring. I predict you will only want the missionary position, no sex toys, no threesomes, no lesbians, bondage or flagellation"

"So true Yvan you got it in one, apart from the sex toys, but to quote the Beatles you'll get 'Love, love love. Love is all you need"

"You only bought a sex toy for me Feef, not one for yourself"

"It's cos I think the chemicals in the rubber may give me a cancer"

"That's an upsetting thought"

"At the moment all I'm trying to protect is the duration of my life. I certainly don't want a sex toy giving me rectal cancer. Just isn't worth it" Yvan considered what Fi had said, then looked agitated

"If the GMC allow the sex perverts to work and they continue to practise and can't keep their minds, hands and body parts under control they should recommend a good daily dose of 'Mama's ruler treatment'. That should work" Yvan said looking amused and disgusted. "No more upward pointings after that. In fact there may never be another siting of 'little Johnny'. He will stay little."

"There is one more bit of information I need to give you Yvan which may help in deciding whether you think like a man or a woman. I took your advice about writing everything we talked about as a sequel to my book "Murder in Medicine" and did some research for my next book " Sex in Medicine" I found two fascinating cases about Gender identity. One supports my view that you are born male or female but listen to them both and see what you think."

26. MALE /FEMALE REPULSIVE SEX ASSIGNMENT

In the mid-1960s David Reimer was born a biological male but suffered irreparable damage to his penis as an infant due to a failed circumcision. Psychologist John Money encouraged gender reassignment of David to be brought up as a girl. Reimer's parents were advised to raise Reimer as a girl. Reimer underwent surgery as an infant to construct rudimentary female genitals, and was given female hormones during puberty.

"Was he ever told he was a guy?"

"No. During childhood, Reimer was never told he was biologically male and regularly visited Money, who tracked the progress of his gender reassignment."

"He was experimenting?"

"Reimer was unknowingly acting as an experimental subject in Money's controversial investigation, which he called the John/Joan case. The case provided results that were used to justify thousands of sex reassignment surgeries for cases of children with reproductive abnormalities."

"Was his work correct? Was he right?"

"No. Despite his upbringing, Reimer rejected the female identity as a young teenager and began living as a male. He suffered severe depression throughout his life, which culminated in his suicide at thirty-eight years old."

"Did Money get away scot free?"

"You must read the rest of this article yourself Yvan because it makes me very, very angry that bastards like that in medicine with their own arrogant bullshit can destroy the life of a young man and base their preposterous gender identity research work on a single experiment that went wrong There are probably many others who have suffered as a result of Money's work.

Yvan looked up the rest of the Reimer story on the Internet . Fi was bullishly refusing to discuss it any further. Her body language signified her displeasure at even being asked to consider the subject anymore.

Yvan looked it up and realised he felt the same extreme displeasure when he read the whole saga.

Reimer, and his public statements about the trauma of his transition, brought attention to gender identity and called into question the sex reassignment of infants and children.

Bruce Peter Reimer was born on 22 August 1965 in Winnipeg, Ontario, to Janet and Ron Reimer. At six months of age, both Reimer and his identical twin, Brian, were diagnosed with phimosis, a condition in which the foreskin of the penis cannot retract, inhibiting regular urination. On 27 April 1966, Reimer underwent circumcision, a common procedure in which a physician surgically removes the foreskin of the penis. Usually, physicians performing circumcisions use a scalpel or other sharp instrument to remove foreskin. However, Reimer's physician used the unconventional technique of cauterization, or burning to cause tissue death. Reimer's circumcision failed. Reimer's brother did not

Reimer's brother did not undergo circumcision and his phimosis healed naturally. While the true extent of Reimer's penile damage was unclear, the overwhelming majority of biographers and journalists maintained that it was either totally severed or otherwise damaged beyond the possibility of function.

In 1967, Reimer's parents sought the help of John Money, a psychologist and sexologist who worked at the Johns Hopkins Hospital in Baltimore, Maryland. In the mid twentieth century, Money helped establish the views on the psychology of gender identities and roles. In his academic work, Money argued in favor of the increasingly mainstream idea that gender was a societal construct, malleable from an early age. He stated that being raised as a female was in Reimer's interest, and recommended sexual reassignment surgery. At the time, infants born with abnormal or intersex genitalia commonly received such interventions.

Following their consultation with Money, Reimer's parents decided to raise Reimer as a girl. Physicians at the Johns Hopkins Hospital removed Reimer's testes and damaged penis, and constructed a vestigial vulvae and a vaginal canal in their place. The physicians also opened a small hole in Reimer's lower abdomen for urination. Following his gender reassignment surgery, Reimer was given the first name Brenda, and his parents raised him as a girl. He received estrogen during adolescence to promote the development of breasts. Throughout his childhood, Reimer was not informed about his male biology.

Throughout his childhood, Reimer received annual checkups from Money. His twin brother was also part of Money's research on sexual development and gender in children. As identical twins growing up in the same family, the Reimer brothers were what Money considered ideal case subjects for a psychology study on gender. Reimer was the first documented case of sex reassignment of a child born developmentally normal, while Reimer's brother was a control subject who shared Reimer's genetic makeup, intrauterine

the Reimer brothers were what Money considered ideal case subjects for a psychology study on gender. Reimer was the first documented case of sex reassignment of a child born developmentally normal, while Reimer's brother was a control subject who shared Reimer's genetic makeup, intrauterine space, and household.

During the twin's psychiatric visits with Money, and as part of his research, Reimer and his twin brother were directed to inspect one another's genitals and engage in behavior resembling sexual intercourse. Reimer claimed that much of Money's treatment involved the forced reenactment of sexual positions and motions with his brother. In some exercises, the brothers rehearsed missionary positions with thrusting motions, which Money justified as the rehearsal of healthy childhood sexual exploration. In his Rolling Stone interview, Reimer recalled that at least once, Money photographed those exercises. Money also made the brothers inspect one another's pubic areas. Reimer stated that Money observed those exercises both alone and with as many as six colleagues. Reimer recounted anger and verbal abuse from Money if he or his brother resisted orders, in contrast to the calm and scientific demeanor Money presented to their parents. Reimer and his brother underwent Money's treatments at preschool and grade school age. Money described Reimer's transition as successful, and claimed that Reimer's girlish behavior stood in stark contrast to his brother's boyishness. Money reported on Reimer's case as the John/Joan case, leaving out Reimer's real name. For over a decade, Reimer and his brother unknowingly provided data that, according to biographers and the Intersex Society of North America, was used to reinforce Money's theories on gender fluidity and provided justification for thousands of sex reassignment surgeries for children with abnormal genitals.

Contrary to Money's notes, Reimer reports that as a child he experienced severe gender dysphoria, a condition in which someone experiences distress as a result of their assigned gender. Reimer reported that he did not identify as a girl and resented Money's visits for treatment. At the age of thirteen, Reimer threatened to commit suicide if his parents took him to Money on the next annual visit. Bullied by peers in school for his masculine traits, Reimer claimed that despite receiving female hormones, wearing dresses, and having his interests directed toward typically female norms, he always felt that he was a boy. In 1980, at the age of fifteen, Reimer's father told him the truth about his birth and the subsequent procedures. Following that revelation, Reimer assumed a male identity, taking the first name David. By age twenty-one, Reimer had received testosterone therapy and surgeries to remove his breasts and reconstruct a penis. He married Jane Fontaine, a single mother of three, on 22 September 1990.

In adulthood, Reimer reported that he suffered psychological trauma due to Money's experiments, which Money had used to justify sexual reassignment surgery for children with intersex or damaged genitals since the 1970s. In the mid-1990s, Reimer met Milton Diamond, a psychologist at the University of Hawaii, in Honolulu, Hawaii, and academic rival of Money. Reimer participated in a follow-up study conducted by Diamond, in which Diamond catalogued the failures of Reimer's transition.

In 1997, Reimer began speaking publicly about his experiences, beginning with his participation in Diamond's study. Reimer's first interview appeared in the December 1997 issue of Rolling Stone magazine. In interviews, and a later book about his experience, Reimer described his interactions with Money as torturous and abusive. Accordingly, Reimer claimed he developed a lifelong distrust of hospitals and medical professionals.

With those reports, Reimer caused a multifaceted controversy over Money's methods, honesty in data reporting, and the general ethics of sex reassignment surgeries on infants and children. Reimer's description of his childhood conflicted with the scientific consensus about sex reassignment at the time. According to NOVA, Money led scientists to believe that the John/Joan case demonstrated an unreservedly successful sex transition. Reimer's parents later blamed Money's methods and alleged surreptitiousness for the psychological illnesses of their sons, although the notes of a former graduate student in Money's lab indicated that Reimer's parents dishonestly represented the transition's success to Money and his coworkers. Reimer was further alleged by supporters of Money to have incorrectly recalled the details of his treatment. On Reimer's case, Money publicly dismissed his criticism as antifeminist and anti-trans bias, but, according to his colleagues, was personally ashamed of the failure.

In his early twenties, Reimer attempted to commit suicide twice. According to Reimer, his adult family life was strained by marital problems and employment difficulty. Reimer's brother, who suffered from depression and schizophrenia, died from an antidepressant drug overdose in July of 2002. On 2 May 2004, Reimer's wife told him that she wanted a divorce. Two days later, at the age of thirty-eight, Reimer committed suicide by firearm.

Reimer, Money, and the case became subjects of numerous books and documentaries following the exposé. Reimer also became somewhat iconic in popular culture, being directly referenced or alluded to in the television shows Chicago Hope, Law & Order, and Mental. The BBC series Horizon covered his story in two episodes, "The Boy Who Was Turned into a Girl" (2000) and "Dr.

Money and the Boy with No Penis" (2004). Canadian rock group 'The Weaker thans' wrote "Hymn of the Medical Oddity" about Reimer, and the New York-based Ensemble Studio Theatre production Boy was based on Reimer's life.

"That is a very sad story Fi."

"What are your thoughts?"

"Bloody doctors get it wrong all the time Fi. That is what I think. They should not be unleashed on unsuspecting patients with their arrogance."

"Poor Reimer. The doctors experimenting like that on him. No wonder he killed himself."

"I'd have difficulty living with a man who thinks he is a woman inside but someone who has been forced into being a woman when he was a man. That would be hell for both parties."

"What was the other case?"

"Dealing with this particular sexual matter makes me ill Yvan but I will tell you about the next case because the guy is a journalist Richard Hoskins and wrote his own story."

"I think I've read his articles?"

"Before we proceed Yvan lets look up the film "The Boy Who Was Turned Into a Girl," which was a documentary, directed by Andrew Cohen about Reimer's life (BBC, 2000.)

"Is he related to you Yvan?"

"Cohen is a common surname Fi. Unless my parents were up to something and I never knew about it."

"Richard Hoskins flew to Bangkok in 2016 for operations to transition from a man to a female. I am not sure what part this has to play in his decisions but in October 2009 his son David who was, 19, climbed an electricity pylon and reached for a 33k volt cable. The son of his first wife died in Dec   but his second marriage ended following his son's death and Richard turned to his feminine side.

"It all sounds strange Fi. What were the reasons for wanting new identity?

"I guess it depends on what was going on in that household? We will never know." The reasons were complex and unrelated to male or female gender but Richard says 'Coming back to my true self as Richard was one of the greatest things I ever did'

"Good place to go to explore true identity? Lady boy land."

"I've always thought Thai men were effeminate"

"He went for his operations with a companion Jenny but he didn't discuss it with her and at the last moment he changed his mind."

"Was he suffering from gender confusion at all?

"He had no need to transition Yvan. For many years he had been living an apparently contented life as a man

"Was he? Or did he want to experience the male sex?"

"It was nothing to do with sex. he was never attracted to men, but it was something that he wanted quite powerfully all the same. He wanted to put on make-up, to wear female clothes and wanted to step into the ladies' loos."

" Well he could do that and just pretend to be a woman"

"No he wanted to be female. He bought some stuff from Vanuatu on the internet and almost immediately his breasts began to grow but within weeks he was regretting it, however."

"Why didn't he just go to his GP and confess?".

"He did. And it was from that point onwards that he found himself enmeshed in the National Health Service gender identity machine."

"What happened?"

"It's not as simple as changing sex. Conventionally, someone wishing to change sex should wait two years before being prescribed life-changing hormones – an entirely sensible rule. The system bends over backwards for anyone who wants to transition.

"They obviously made a mistake as he changed his mind"

"Not before he took 18 months of NHS-prescribed medications testosterone blockers and oestrogens."

"The man is an idiot. What a waste of NHS money."

"The state also paid for him to undergo 80 hours of extremely painful electrolysis on his face."

"I'd like my stubble systematically plucked out so I wouldn't have to shave".

"You would not like that Yvan. Having my pubes waxed kills me and I do it every 3 months."

"So what does he do next?"

"He has massive facial reconstructive surgery in Thailand. The surgery took nine hours and was a process of quite astonishing brutality. Forehead reconstruction around the orbital rims, to make them more almond shaped. He had his face peeled away from his skull and had neck and cheek liposuction. He paid £15,00 for the price."

"At least he wasn't wasting NHS money."

"The person who should pay is his teacher who abused him as a child"

"I knew there was something coming. There is always some trauma What happened to the teacher?"

"He got a ten-year sentence for sexual abuse."

"I'm so glad Richard Hoskins didn't have the full transformations. I hope he is happy now" Yvan exchanged a glance and a nod with Fi as she said

"What do you make of it?"

"I think he has a hidden story Fi related to why his son climbed the electric pylon. That story has not been told here Fi or anywhere else. It has gone to bed with his son's death"

"I thought the same Yvan. Let's go to Gretna Green tomorrow and get married before I discover anything more about sex mad doctors nurses and the like. I want a straight and uncomplicated life with a guy like you"

"What sort of guy is that Fi my Dorogoy?"

"Someone who has loved and stood by me and not asked much at all times. Ready to give and never take. A constant source of support through all the times. Yes I know you. Yvan you are my darling Dorogoy as I am yours."

"YA tebya lyublyu Fi"

"And I love you too Yvan."

LIST OF PUNISHMENTS FOR OFFENCES

1. Theepa Sundaraligam - $16,000 Canadian dollars towards the patient's therapy and $6,000 in costs to the college.

2. Mohammad Ihsan - Erasure from the medical register. Cannot work as a doctor again

3. Abizer Sakarwala -   suspended from working; registered sex offender

4. Suganthan Kayilasathanandan - license revoked paid $ 46,220 to college. Cannot work without a license

5. Jonathan Mark Fielden - struck off register. Sentenced to 5 months imprisonment suspended for 12 months. Ordered to carry out 150 hours of unpaid work and pay costs of £3,500. Must attend 30 Rehabilitation Activity requirements. Unable to work as a doctor in this country.

6. Dirk Redman - struck off the medical register by the High Court. Unable to work as a doctor

7. Myles Bradbury - struck off register. Jailed for 16 years.

8. Cristian Bogdan- sanction of erasure. Cannot work in UK as a doctor. Ordered to complete 150 hours of unpaid work and made subject to a Sexual Harm Prevention Order for 10 years.

9. Adrian Marsden - Struck off register. Fined £2,500 and 5 years sexual harm prevention order, and 18 month community order. Pays £ 85 costs and £ 85 victim surcharge.

10.   Jonathan Walsh - Struck off.   Sexual harm prevention order. Sex offender register for life. Computer equipment destroyed. Jailed for 3 years

11. Stuart Creed - Struck off

12. David Jones - Completes ethics and boundaries course at his expense. Pays costs amounting to $10,180 to the College.

13. Rupert Pemsel - 10 months suspension from work. Returns to practice as a GP not a Hospital doctor.

14. Robert Barnett - Struck off. Pays £7,000 legal costs

15. Ana Maria Gonzalez-Angulo - 10 years in prison and a $10,000 fine

16. Nicholas Salway - Struck off

17.Manish Shah.- Jail with 3 life sentences. 15 years minimum

18. George Tyndall - Not licensed anymore

19. Ian Newby - 14 week prison sentence suspended for 1 year. Paid £1250 in compensation and an £85 victim surcharge. Loses job"

20. Thomas Jenkins - Struck off medical register. Takes part in a sex offenders' programme for three years. Placed on the sex offenders register for five years.

21. Steven Ashenford - Struck off medical register

22. Adam Osborne - Struck off medical register

23. Lam Hoe Yeoh - Jailed for five years . Struck off medical register

24. Stanislaw Franciszek Zulichoswk - Struck off. Cannot work in UK as a doctor. Returns to Poland

25. Gordon Carter - Struck off register

26. Maurice Ripley - Struck off register

27. Iftekhar Ahmed - Struck off register. May be practicing in America

28. Carl Tanzler - Crime reported out of date so no punishment

29. Fred Janke - Struck off

30. Nicholas Spicer - Allowed to go back to work in another part of the country following a six-month ban.

31. Dr Palaniappan Saravanan- Suspended immediately. Sacked by hospital. Struck off register.

32. Julian Proctor - Struck off register. Cannot work as a doctor in UK

33. Leendert Verstraten- Suspended immediately from work. Then struck off.

34. Christopher Ball-Nossa- Struck off

3. David Simon revocation of license in Florida. Similar to being struck off

If a doctor or licensed health care professional is struck off the medical register in the UK it is entirely possible that they can turn up in another country and continue to work. Be warned if they are somewhere else and working.